I0829795

The Reality Pirate's Guide to Your Paranormal Normal

ZOLI ALTHEA BROWNE
D.Div, PhD, D.S.M., PhD

Contents

To All My Mothers

To Helen, who gave me life

To Ruth, who gave me A life

To V, who awaits my return

And to Sophia, who lives within us all

zoliartexoticamontana.com/music
"Songs for Mother Nature"

Introduction to the Unseen World

You are surrounded by energies and activities, both seen and unseen. This is God's natural world we share with His other creations. Some say that the world we see, hear, touch, taste, and smell is only 10 percent of what really exists. I don't know if that is true, but I do know there is more out there than we notice. We all share the gift of extra-sensory perception. Some folks seem to be highly attentive and perceptive to the unseen, while others pay it no heed.

Should you learn more about this unseen world? It's up to you, truly. But, I believe that an inner attunement illuminates the outer experience. My hopes are that you gain understanding from what I write. I seek to create consolation rather than desolation, but that comfort is the result of understanding how to navigate the darkness. If some of my writings seem to you peculiar, so be it. Fear is a great teacher. It warns us not to tread heavily in the areas unsuited to us. Please know that the warnings I post refer always to the nature of that which is uncontrollable.

The world of evil and beings seeking to deceive you is indeed real. I believe we are protected by the blood of Christ, the Eucharist, our prayers, and our good deeds. You may have experiences in life which fall under the domain of those icky beings. Ephesians 6:12 reminds us that these are principalities of immense power. Once we encounter them in flesh and blood, we are already touching their wounds. They know our names. I maintain a deep and wary respect for these energies as I would a dangerous animal.

Fools certainly do rush in where the wise refuse to tread. Since I don't know you or your beliefs, I choose to write from my own. I offer sincere apologies to any of you who may take offence at anything I write. *Mea culpa.* I am clarifying my experiences with the light I find in Christ and his works with the wisdom of the Buddha and his gentleness. Because I was raised a Reformed Jew, I still find comfort in some of the Hebrew prayers imprinted on my heart from the first 20 years in this life.

When I had my DNA done, I had neither Ashkenazic nor Sephardic DNA. I believe that God inspired my birth mother to place me with these wonderful people for the countless blessings we shared. In 1953, Louisiana was still under Napoleonic Law. Isn't that crazy? So, there was a law that prevented Jews from adopting non-Jewish children. My birth mother revealed that she had to sign a document giving my Jewish adoptive parents the right to adopt me, a Scottish, British, Swedish kid.

I believe also that, inshallah, God guides our every move. As an ordained metaphysical minister, I believe in the diversity of one world with many beliefs. That is Theosophy. So, when you read that I'm a Jesuit Catholic, that flavour is tempered by a curious temperance and love for humanity. I see people as the illumination of God's world, expressing creativity and seeking to spiritualize matter.

What are you looking for in these pages? I believe in the power of prayer, meditation and service. My prayer for you with my work is that you'll find a bit of what you seek. I do not believe in trying to impress with quotes and with big words. Those words serve well in other venues, but I seek to address you in the same way that I think.

Neither do I seek to convince you that any of this is your particular brand of truth. What are you looking for? I believe the Kingdom is indeed within us. Maybe my writings can remind you that your experiences are real. You matter. Your experiences are valued. Please accept these as my love written and given to you. There is a prayer called the Hoʻoponopono prayer. It says, "I love you, I'm sorry, please forgive me, thank you." The Hoʻoponopono addresses the grace and dignity of forgiveness.

This ancient Hawaiian prayer melts karmic negativity and blesses new ground for moving past problems with oneself and others. A psychiatrist at a prison for the criminally insane began saying this prayer over his patient charts. He experienced a calmer population. When we say this prayer for self-forgiveness, we will find a lessening of bad feelings. When one says it towards the other, relationships often improve. I offer you this prayer said to you as a request for anything I might write that you find offensive.

In these pages, you will find stories and lessons from my experiences so you can embrace your paranormal normal. Throughout the book, there are sections where some of your questions are answered. If you have others, please get in touch.

The whole concept of reality pirate is a state of being, not a person to strive to be like. Everyone is themselves; stay grounded in the physical world and then come back. Because reality is not what it used to be, it can be helpful to follow the Reality Pirate's (RP) guide. The Reality Pirate concept is a way to explore other ways of being. RP has experiences which we will delve into in another book.

My experience is not yours. When I look in the mirror, I see me, not you. Indeed, my love for humanity and my aspiration to share validity in my stories require an understanding of boundaries between us. I have too much respect for you and your beliefs, for that is love. Go in peace!

zoliartexoticamontana.com/music
"Inner Child"

Your Questions Answered: Who is the Reality Pirate?

A reality pirate is an entity ensouled in a physical body who consciously pirates from one reality to another, sometimes at a fast pace. Reality pirates are different from reality hogs in that the latter are ensouled entities who maintain frequency. They neither shift nor pirate due to glamorous constraints, experiencing life from one point of view only. Tolerance is a requisite of pirating; compassion is its foothold in any reality.

The Reality Pirate supports those interested in the expansion of consciousness and the ethical dissemination of alternative frequency receptions. The Reality Pirate offers information in the areas of UFOs and ETs, psychology and psychiatry, Devic and animal consciousness, interpersonal relations, codependency, addiction and interdimensional physics. All of us at the Reality Pirate, those in bodies and out, desire that you read our words with zetetic discernment and an open heart.

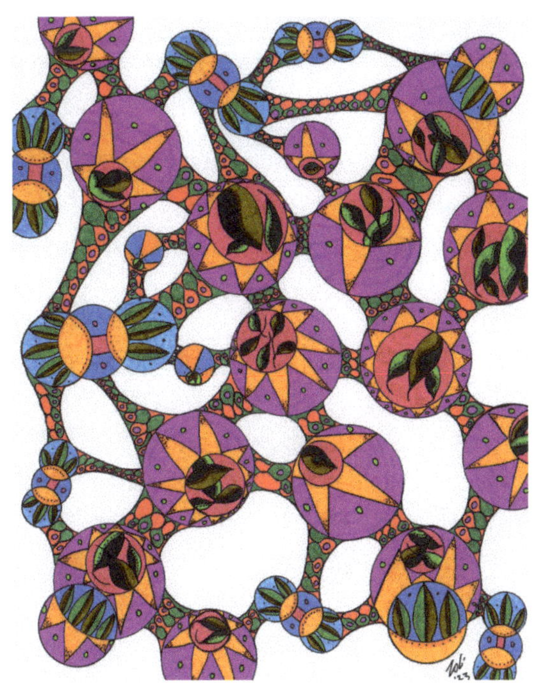

Chapter 1:
Portals Connecting Dimensions

There is so much that I have read and continue to read that I would love to include here, but that would not be fair. What I am charged to do by those who guard and guide me is to present to you in my own words what I understand these things to be. Discernment is a requisite of reading others' interpretations of reality, so please do that. I suggest you do the research yourself. I do try, however, to be as accurate as possible. I love the idea of portals and their potential in 3D reality.

A portal is an opening in the fabric of third-dimensional reality. We agree to live in 3D with all its limitations and wonders. What does that mean? Portals are doorways and windows allowing things from here to go somewhere else and things from somewhere else to show up here. The naked eye does not see it, nor does one physically hear it. Your spider senses, though, can oftentimes feel that there is a disturbance in the force.

Can we all do that? Well, it depends on how sensitive you are and how much you have learned to attune to your inner senses.

Those five physical senses are your internal compass to the unseen. Are portals good or bad? It is not the doorway itself, but what it connects to can be awful. Otherworldly beings who use portals can be negative or positive just like here on this plane.

Can you just create a portal? It requires intense focus and emotional directing of your will. Request help, but from whom? You are accompanied at all times by not just your guardian angel, who by the way does not speak with you but just keeps you on the right track, but your guidance group composed of discarnate entities, Devic energies, critters, alien energies, you name it. It appears that these beings are assigned to help, maybe due to your own good deeds or crappy ones. We have all got 'em! They may be people who have passed over, who love you and are in between lives.

> *Portals are doorways and windows allowing things from here to go somewhere else and things from somewhere else to show up here.*

Lots of ideas, thoughts, and feelings emanate from these same beings. The high beings may or may not be attuned to you or you to them. Here are my ideas on this. You know how goofy we can all be on vacations. We wear funny hats, act out of character, and gawk at what locals are bored with. I think interdimensional visitors can pop through a portal and present the same thing.

They can be like goofy tourists at West Yellowstone at the bottom of our state of Montana. Tourists try to ride Buffalo, get selfies with apex predators, and wash socks in thermal pools ad nauseam. They do it because they are unfamiliar with the specific signatures of the area. We hear of crazy people doing crazy stuff. It seems that human nature is not just for humans.

Can you tell where a portal is? Usually not. I really don't know that much about it, so I'll refer you to the online plethora of experts or at least people who think they are. I can, however, define areas of portals when they reoccur in my familiar environments.

Weirdness interrupts my life at all costs. What's not weird is what we're used to, right? Sometimes, we like it, and other times, it's awful. Portals can appear and disappear. I really don't get that, but it's true. Energy is the one constant working through all realities.

I don't know about you, but I expect things to work. When I walk into a room, I expect to be able to interact with what's there. When I'm supposed to be somewhere at 2 o'clock, I expect the clock to say 2 o'clock, and when I walk in, it's actually 2 o'clock. So-called things are supposed to work to offer consistency. When we make plans, they're expected to work out. Times and places are dependent upon stability, so what about the time warps, portals and temporal-spatial discontinuums? The auditory and visual media are ripe with examples, now captured and available to be heard and viewed from your living room.

Are they real? I like to think that the powers that be, the karmic overlords and the ones pushing the buttons controlling time and space are a dependable lot. It must take an act of God to prevent leaks, breaks, and warps from disrupting our human world. They care about us, our sanity and our addiction to consistency, true dat. But is that the only truth? Are they cryptoid visitors from these dimensions? Are they from another fabric of time popping through portals? Do otherworldly beings pop in and out of rips in the fabric? I don't know, but I think they do.

What we notice and what we miss are not always, well, conscious, are they? The fabric of the third dimension really is fraught with rips, intentionally placed or not. There's that dichotomy again. One thing is absolutely real, and the other one is not, but occurring simultaneously. Just thinking about it drives me nuts. Perhaps it's all about trust, the agreements we make in order to work on Earth and commune with the reality of life. What do you think? What if you went to the store, came back and found it was ten years later? That's the stuff of movies, right? We depend on time and space to work together, but I think these time-space discrepancies are more common than we perceive.

What if we just go with them unconsciously, allowing shifts in and out of the dimensional world and the density? When one says that's impossible, we have reached the glass ceiling of our own experiences. I think I'll just go watch a Western and binge on sci-fi.

zoliartexoticamontana.com/music
"Dream Direction"

Your Questions Answered: When did you first understand the nature of portals?

I started hearing about portals when I was running the Center of Melchizedek in Nashville back in the late seventies. The word was floating around, though I didn't really know what it was. I read about them, but I didn't experience them fully until I moved to the farm. The space brothers spoke of them, and people in the new age community spoke of them. I found that there were areas at the farm that were definite portals. And I didn't know if I had set them or if the Devics had, or the space brothers.

I think a lot of things work like that where we hear about something, and we kind of file it away. But I think it takes a direct experience with things, for me at least, to be able to cognate it and for visuals to get formed around it. At the farm, I had countless experiences with the portals that were there, and they would change and move. It was quite intriguing.

Experiencing something makes them more understandable. The only way that I can write about something is if I have experienced it. Otherwise, if it's something I have read, it's somebody else's words. So, I choose to connect everything I've written, and I'm writing about with my own personal experience because I can guarantee that, for me, that was true.

I have to be authentic. When I went through my channeling phase, which was one of the steps to get me up to where I could work through my heart, it took twenty years to get me there. But during that stage, I depended very much on what other people were saying and their definitions of things because I was in a school. Sooner or later, the student has to become a teacher.

The beings that guard and guide me, they absolutely say, if they tell me something or if I read something in *Share International* magazine or Theosophy and think that is an amazing concept, they won't let me write about that. They want me to sit on it and let it cook until I can experience it. Then I can connect that, then I can write about it. And I think I'm pressing people to honor their own experience. I'm working with a young girl right now who's fifty years younger than me. She's twenty. Just a bright mind. She's never been exposed to this. So, I have to speak with her for hours on end about my experience and my interpretation of that.

I don't want her to take that this is God's truth. But we kind of have to. That's what is difficult. We have to take that as a truth until we know differently. So, I recommend you check with your heart and your gut, but that takes practice too. My mom used to say to me, "Be who you are, just be yourself."

And I'd say, "But I don't know who that is. How can I, to my own self be true if I don't know?"

And she would say, "Well, that's your life journey."

This can take a lifetime. And I think that is the soul level that's revealed. These words that were given like portals or astral realms, any of these definitions: if we just intellectually know those things are not experiential, and to me, they're real. They're valid, like sitting in a class and getting definitions, but I like to lead myself and others to find experiences with those things firsthand. And you will. It will happen.

Chapter 2:
Purpose, Light, and Collective Energy

Who we are and what we are can be quite different. Think about that. Goodness does not naturally prevail on Earth. We must invoke it in His name as a requirement of life. Only through love for each other and ourselves can the light activate His power to us and through us. Do things always happen for a reason? I don't think so. But we can make reason out of what happens. Detachment and adaptability are areas I can certainly improve upon in my own life.

I am not a city gal. I prefer the homey, laid-back lifestyle of the countryside. But cities actually have more chi energy than the countryside. New York City is one of the seven chakras of the planet. The chi energy there is electric. I find it peculiar that in these days of Aquarian feminine energy that technology is so apparent. Constant internet connection blocks our feeling nature, the terminally online.

When we spend most of our waking hours looking down into a piece of plastic, what does this say about our culture? Well, it's the good and the bad. Things change, don't they? Do you think all thoughts express as emotions, or do emotions come first and create the thought? Do we feel emotions because of what we just thought? Our external experiences are what we notice with our five physical senses. The visualizing of thoughts creates an emotion, right? Emotions are always connected to what we were thinking.

Everything is in the present, even though we get stuck in the past or busy ourselves planning or worrying about the future. I was as you are. You will be who I am. Death is inevitable—*memento mori*—so seize the day and take advantage of being here.

The Reality Pirate brings you to the present. Spend some time there figuring yourself out, and you will begin to understand and accept those around you. If we are ourselves, we will be able to manage our fears and the unknown.

> *We use our personal densities to impinge upon the experiences of others. We are boundary violators and perpetrators of running over others' free will. We just don't seem to know any better.*

We use our personal densities to impinge upon the experiences of others. We are boundary violators and perpetrators running over others' free will. We just don't seem to know any better. I hate it when I do that. Densities are personal; dimensions are universal. We fight what we don't understand with the spare tools we learn from other battles, forcing a veiled victory over the enemies of our own desires. When I look into the mirror, I see myself, not somebody else.

Boundaries are a learned skill and a kindness born from feeling the effects of having none with ourselves or others. I write my experiences. I try not to quote. My literary boundaries separate my style from that of writers quoting other sources and opining on them. That is their work. It's magnificent, but it's not mine. Indeed, I sometimes refer to religious and spiritual sources, but these references align my experience with said topics. I'm a prolific producer of my own creativity in music, art, and writing. Where is your creative spark? Some folks say they are not creative, but creativity is more than expressing the arts!

If I remain true to my boundaries, I'll avoid courting others to validate what I have to say. I'm guided to stay in my own lane. My insecurities tease me into thin spaces when I actually do very well staying true to myself and my work.

When we speak of community, we consider how we gather as a whole to find common ground. There's truly little more difficult than trying to agree in a group. As we aspire to solutions for the good of the whole, we secretly harbor egoic ideas and ideals. We all do this internally, although not all is selfishly expressed.

Have you ever considered the thousands of potential external stimuli we are surrounded by in, let's say, just one hour? Look at the natural world, the man-made objects, the voices, the scents, the sounds.

We gather in the hopes of solving issues affecting all while expressing what has and has not worked. Ideally, we should be authentic, expressing our true selves without concern for how we appear to others. But come on, we're just people. This is not to be judgmental, rude, and uncaring, but an expression of who and what we are from our hearts, rarely done, especially during these uncertain times. In my experiences with groups, we tend to attach onto like-minded others.

We seek affirmation of our own desires and support for our own beliefs. No two of us are exactly alike. Each can offer brilliance or ignorance. We present our projections, our unexpressed fears and our methods learned in childhood of how we manipulate to get our way. We also use what worked for goodness.

How do we even focus on one thing? Community is like that. Each member lives in their own personal world, as well as our shared world. That personal world is a density. That is consciousness connected.

zoliartexoticamontana.com/music
"Arabic Eyes"

Your Questions Answered: How can we tap into the collective energy?

We don't do anything on our own, really. We're all collective energy. We're the whole. There are sixty billion souls waiting to be incarnated. And them, plus those of us who are in body, are all really one soul, actually. We divide into these little sparks of light. We come down, and we gather experience, and we take it back to the fold, like the Borg in a way, but we do have individual consciousness. It's one of those dichotomies that I think we really can't understand: How two things can be true in their opposite.

It's an individual thing, and it feels lonely because it's supposed to. I spend a lot of time alone. I have to be alone to do my work. I'm an empath. When I go out into the world, I pick everything up, and so I have to control that and accept that. In order to do my work, I have to be alone, but am I really alone? Heck, no, I'm surrounded by beings as we all are, but they're in different dimensions, different densities. We're never really alone in that way.

It's a dichotomy.

Chapter 3:
My Process as a Psychic Medium

What is my process? I don't dissociate and fall into a trance. I am taught to remain conscious and be responsible for what I say and hear. However, others report that I sometimes say things I do not recall. That is being in an altered state. Trance mediumship was all the rage in the 1800s. From the Fox sisters to Madame Blavatsky to the Bailey work later on, these actions addressed mediumship in different ways. However, Bailey and Blavatsky did not fall into a deep trance. They were taught to be conscious mediums. I call this MEDIATING FREQUENCY. The beings I have worked with over the years began using a specific vocabulary to define our work. They use the word frequency to define these states and discernable shifts. I choose to think that I mediate, and it comes from the sixth chakra, the Ajna center, from the heart also, which is the fourth energy center. But it has taken me fifty years to get here, right? And yes, I'm still learning more about my process.

Once your energy can reach the heart, it will shoot up to the fifth chakra and that chakra is for communication and speaking your truth from the heart. From there, it goes to the sixth chakra, the Ajna center, which is part of your intuition up to the seventh chakra and out through the head to the eighth and on. I won't delve into that. There are tomes written on those processes. What we're concerned with here is how the heck do I do what I do? I see things.

I see full-color movies play out in my mind's eye. I've had to train myself to believe what I see is real, from God, from spirit and from my soul. If I try to make it up, the movie stops and pauses, it freezes, and I feel it in my third chakra emotional center. That area in your stomach houses the emotions and Astral energies.

The mind and gut emotions will lie to you, while the heart never will. I have worked hard for the ability to discern between the gut emotions and what is generated from my heart and Ajna, sixth chakra, third eye.

Sometimes I think I'm smelling the movie but have discerned that the nasal center of smell is connected to the physical center of the sixth chakra, the intuitive Ajna center. Those energetic messages are mental, very crisp, and clear. I'm usually surprised by what comes out. I can't make this stuff up! There's feeling connected to it, but it's unemotional. I'll tell you something funny that started about five years ago. When waiting at a stoplight, I would say, "Three, two, one, go!"

The light changes from red to green. I thought I was smelling it. I can't always do this but when I do it, I say I'm on. When I can't do it, I'm off. I thought I was smelling this, but the scent was not involved. The intention is that I'm connecting my energy field to the electromagnetics of the light. It's through the sixth chakra, the Ajna center, intuition. And that is where I thought I smelled it from, but it wasn't a smell, see? It was connected to the nasal cavities in an inner sensory way.

I pray and invoke often, "Lord, not my will but Thine be done to me and through me, may my will be Thine." At times, I experience moment-by-moment synchronicity, unexpected and out of the control of my conscious mind. As a psychic medium, I am trained to allow the peculiarities of superphysical messages to lead me from one moment to the next. We exist in a supernatural world, manifesting the five physical senses in the natural world. I am on a need-to-know basis because His will, God's will, controls the outcome.

When I align my will with His, things go well for me. If not, fate just takes over. I am often and usually disheartened, frustrated, fearful and unconfident because I cannot see where I am led. I wonder, is this what the best path is for me, and is my path the best for others? I live in a holding pattern until several factors make themselves known through communications from people or experiences in the physical world. The physical world, sooner or later, usually later, offers visual, auditory, and physical confirmations as the movie reveals its passage through time.

My only goal is that I do what I came here to do. What did my soul and Guidance design for me to do here? God's will can place me in situations to accomplish this, and it's not often fun. I think we work in collaboration with Him. What else is there, truly? I think God's plan is presented to me in His time, but I must act. His plan appears suddenly or languidly, passing me through countless emotions coloring the experiences leading to the final piece. What this means is that human experience creates His world for me to explore my talents for the benefit of service.

When synchronicities begin, they come in at lightning speed. I try to connect them but often miss the mark because, at first, I don't see where they connect. I become disheartened and frustrated, often blaming myself for not getting the point immediately. But that's my Aries sun sign with Mars in the first house and a Grand Trine in Fire. Calm down, Zoli. Once my mind is more placid, I intuit the tendrils of connection between the synchronicities. If I'm in a good mood that day, I will feel my heart chakra radiating with gratitude and magic. Otherwise, I'm just stuck.

Welcome to Earth. The truth is that His world becomes tangible and real within the space-time reality of physical life. This third dimension becomes colored with other densities and higher frequency realities as He works his plans. At times, the presence of God's plan presents itself with deep grace, like a soft perfume wafting through an open window from a garden just outside.

These are the moments of perfect silence when time seems to stop. These moments offer me hope and reassurance that He is indeed present always. As deep blue ice melts, the liquidity transforms into translucence. So do our souls become clear with the passing of emotional and physical death. But more on that later.

I continue to experience the world as a movie of sorts. When I see things, I'm given information about them. I often see graphs or signs above the visions which reveal to me their raison d'être. Last night, as I sat in bed pondering the beings in my life, I saw a familiar one walk through the bedroom suite to plop down unceremoniously in the chair next to the sauna. I certainly knew and recognized her as a rather constant companion. I feel her presence more often than I attune to her form.

She is rather stout, about five foot seven, and looks like Madame Blavatsky, presenting the same serious and rather unkempt demeanor. She is always serious and focused only on the work. I know she is connected to Theosophy, perhaps British or American, in her recent incarnation. Whenever I see her, I'm a bit taken aback by her gruff and unsocial nature. She feels like a friend whose purpose with me is fully focused on keeping the work flowing. She's always garbed in brown hues, has blue eyes, and wears her hair tossed unceremoniously in a loose knot behind her neck.

She is definitely not Blavatsky. Helena passed from Earth to Sirius, where she evolved furiously fast to a point above 4.5 degrees. She is now back on Earth somewhere to become a 5th Degree Master. I remain curious if the work I did in the temporal past led me to the work I do now in this life. It is much harder now than it was then. These centers of light are of the many places working towards the emergence of Maitreya and the Masters of Wisdom.

I remember the late 1970s and 80s in Nashville when I founded and ran my Center of Melchizedek. All of us woo-woo meisters were told to "start a center." There were metaphysical centers and hippie communes popping up all over the place. It was a crazy time. I write often on the cyclic nature of God's work. I call us a terminally online population these days, quite different from those years in Nashville.

As I was driving through town the other day, I got an image of the Blavatsky-looking female who's been around off and on for decades. I became curious about her name. How peculiar that I have never asked these folks what I should call them. They are as familiar to me as my own energy, so an introduction never seemed necessary, right?

"What is your name, my friend?" I asked as I stopped at the light.

Immediately, I heard, "Margo."

Margo?! I psychically heard that, but it didn't make sense. I would never have associated her with that name because all the Margos I have known were tall, blonde, lithe, Swedish-looking, and beautiful.

But the ability to believe what we hear psychically is a learned skill. If I feel something below the fourth chakra, I have learned that there is fear, deception or simple glamour involved. But if the intuition is working, it is centered above the heart somewhere, usually around the throat trachea and Ajna center.

All material expressions seek recognition and acceptance of their beinghood. Angels, demons, fairies, and other such beings don't have physical bodies though. They are pure spirit, fluid. The Devic kingdoms possess forms not of this world. Tree spirits, for example, may show themselves in their leaves, branches, or bark in a form recognizable to humans, maybe as a face. I often, rather hourly, see supernatural forms appear in the most unexpected of places: the shadow formed by a curtain, the natural etchings on stone, prints in a rug, smudges in the mirror. The list is limited only by my ability to see and recognize them. It is way cool! Imagination is image in action. It presses into consciousness the absolute love from God's created world. The signs are there for all who have eyes to see. That which has no form will form in the molecules of physical things so that we can see them. Remember that. The invisible world shows itself to us by slowing down atoms and molecules in physical objects to be reassembled in the shape they want.

That shape can be an animal, a being, or an object. When this happens, there is a discernible energy shift, a specific signature of the event I experience segmentally. Here is an example of how God's world unfolds. Yesterday, I sat working on an art piece, not paying much attention to the TV's background noisc. Thc show playing was a supernatural drama. I heard snippets of conversations but caught the word "goblin" amid the chatter. But this is how the events begin for me. I sense a familiar energy signature and latch onto the word or image presented.

Several hours later, I sensed a close presence as I walked down the hall. Sophia Montana, our cat, stared. I tuned in and psychically perceived two goblins in this house. How did I know they were goblins? I felt the full body signature I get when I simply know something. Yep, I've been trained, and it hasn't been pretty. I never doubted it could have been anything else. I knew they were goblins.

A bit later, as I rummaged through a drawer in our master bath, I happened to look out the window and clearly saw two goblin's faces formed in the reflection of a large plant near the tub. It was a bit disconcerting, which is my word now for scary because these two sweethearts resembled shrunken heads. I thanked them for taking on a form I could see and invited them to interact more with the house fairies. A bit later, as I re-entered the master bath to shower, I saw one of these goblins holding something silver.

He or she was about two feet tall. A lot of these guys present as that size and are very friendly. As of today, I have attuned to these goblin energies, but it feels quite alien as though they speak a foreign tongue. They seem instead intent on working with lunar energy and indeed tomorrow is the new moon in Taurus. As you well know, silver is lunar. As an aside, I'll tell you I can't wear anything silver, I can't wear pearls, and I can't wear opals. These things blow out my energy; too similar in frequency to me, I guess.

I read people as most people read books. This brings me great grief and a depth of compassion. The world is truly governed by the few to benefit greed and avarice. The masses come in beholden to their karmic groups and families. Earth school is the most difficult one in our solar system, and recognized way out there as a challenge among challenges. We float on an ocean of addiction, trailing our tender emotions in the waters of avoidance. I live daily with an overwhelming compassion for those stuck in the processes of drug and alcohol addiction.

Why do I feel such compassion? Because I also have walked this path. I do not know all things and am faulted with my performance of the deadly sins affecting me and my choices. My own grief or faultedness stems from my human nature because I can see and feel intuitively that depth of grief is shared with all humanity.

I can face and fix only my own problems. Fear expresses as anger, seeking distance from fear's source through the fine expressions of human nature. Greed is more internal. It stealthily lurks in the shadows as it requires others to admire its appearance of success. The personality seeks its ego gratification through competition. This world is controlled by greed, avarice, fear, the lower three chakras. We humans seem to crave our craziness.

Again, we can presently only scientifically measure solid, liquid, and gas; physical. That is about all science recognizes. But as you recall, there are four levels extending experience into the unseen. There are four levels above solid, liquid and gas we do not yet recognize, and most of this paranormal stuff is in those four levels. Our five physical senses know only solid, liquid and gas. Our physical measurements of science can measure only solid liquid and gas. We miss most of it. For example, we search for living beings on Mars, but that is ridiculous because they're in the etheric, not the physical. And that is true for all of the planets in our solar system.

My etheric sight developed to allow me to perceive and, at times, see and converse telepathically with these otherworldly beings. So, here goes. Yesterday, I sensed the presence of that very large cat in our home. I tuned into the frequency after observing our own cat, Sophia Montana, lying in an area very unusual for her. A huge tiger lay next to her, so I said hello to him. I felt comforted by its presence and realized it was female, and delighted that I could see her vivid orange and black colorings as if it were cartooned; it was so bright. I walked into my closet to put away laundry soon after, turned around, and saw a very large, solid black house cat taking shape in the quilt leaning against my closet door.

What was that? Was that Sir Serval, the Serval cat that even my husband sees around here? I watched my left brain's attempt to tell me I'd imagined the sight, but I had to admit that it was crystal clear. The image displayed in my peripheral vision as I turned around to exit the closet was obvious. I couldn't ignore it. I then attempted to rationalize who it was, wanting to know why it was there ad nauseam. I now think that it was the large black cat who pops in and out of one of the portals in our home, not Sir Serval, but one who has been here for maybe eight years.

In our area of Montana, there have been several feral black cats who visited our property, most of them eaten by predators. We have foxes, coyotes, bald and golden eagles, black bears, bobcats, wolverines, and yes, cougars. The formation he created by gathering molecules from the quilt reminded me how these unseen beings borrow form to create form.

You may be curious about what happened next. Did I continue to see these beings? Is this what happens with me? Did they disappear? It depends. Today, I see no tiger, but yesterday afternoon, when I opened the garage door to let Sophia Montana out in the garage to hunt mice, I was almost knocked over by not only her but the giant tiger who was running with her as they both scrambled through the door. I recalled my surprise at how huge this tigress was, well up to my waist.

My logical left brain kicked in, and I wondered whether she could fit through the small opening as I held the door partially open. I watched myself wonder if she required an open door anyway. Couldn't she just wander through the wall? I was taken aback by my attempt to logic out the psychic events of the day. I'm usually more accepting and playful around these beings that I am attracted to seeing and feeling, both the dead and the Devic or etheric beings, that I think nothing of it.

This is my normal. Another example of how psychic mediumship manifests involves the etheric appearances of the PWBs. That is my term for the people without bodies. One in particular manifests often. These are beings who are either Masters of Wisdom, discarnate beings who guide our choices or Devic beings.

The worlds outside of the physical, live outside of time and space. This is why ghosts seem to be there for years, stuck in a past point, unaware of the passage of time. When we are creatively engaged, we usually do not know how long we've been playing or working. We are extrasensory-focused. This state is more true than our spatial/temporal agreements experienced solely in the third dimension. Above the third dimension, these three fields are fluid and out of rules imposed on time and space.

Indeed, we enter into form to limit the self with the boundaries of time and space. In astrology, this is Capricorn, the keeper of time. In 2,500 years' time, after this age of Aquarius, we enter into the age of Capricorn. Much will be different. By then, most people will have taken the first-degree initiation. Our temporal/spatial focus will be loosened by the flow of heightened consciousness. Beautiful indeed it shall be.

My etheric sight developed to allow me to see and converse telepathically with otherworldly beings. Last night, as I climbed into bed, I saw a familiar dude amble from the portal in our dressing room into the bedroom where I was sitting in bed reading. The portal extends about ten feet from one area to the next. I'll later address some of the experiences I have had in this area, but for now let's focus on last night. The etheric dude walked past me, sank down into the chair seven feet from the foot of Thom's side of the bed, and smiled. I recognized his signature as that of an old friend.

He carries a small staff, is about five foot five and dresses in what I identify as British traveling clothes from the late 1800s. He is kind, reticent, Yoda-like, and always smiling. He pushes my limits because his clear visage is always unavoidable. Very disconcerting. Last night, he gave me pointers and hints on the subject of what he calls "focused visual meditation." He then asked me to focus on the Mother Archetype. Who do I consider my mothers? Who are the women from my developmental years?

What do they all have in common, and how do I now feel about their consistent commanding presence, their ways of being and interacting with me? I recollected these women and spoke to him, telling him that they all represented security, physical care, safety and education. They nurtured me unknowingly at times. I wonder if they ever knew the effect that they had had upon me.

I fell asleep as I continued pondering his questions.

This morning, I awakened extremely disoriented. Ever since yesterday morning, my left ear had been toning furiously. I have been aware of a connection with my star family lately. This morning, my ego personality fumed about why this visiting dude would reveal nothing to me about what I wanted to know about the mothers. What is my purpose with all of this? What can I do to change anything in my life that is bothering me? Of course, these are things we have to figure for ourselves, right? The dichotomy is humorous because the wise Zoli can wait for her to evolve past ego ranting while her ego's psychotic narcissism bloviates its distrust and disdain of patience.

We all have beings who guard and guide us. Consider recurring things in your own life and to whom they are connected. Do you have recurrent images or sounds to note? I wish I could do this on a more consistent basis. Helper beings characteristically appear in our dreams. My experiences are with several females reappearing in telling dreams. Only one appears, Margot, in my waking state. The men usually manifest in the awake state as the females in the sleep, in my reality.

I've been asked how one can diminish the natural fear, our freeze, flight or fight of perceiving non-human entities. My own experiences have hardened me to see them as non-threatening because that has been my experience with 99 percent of them. I still feel disconcerted when they appear because it's shocking to see something appear out of thin air. Our energy fields interact. That's the shock in it. They redefine molecules and atoms to lower that energy to the etheric visible spectrum for us.

Whenever we connect fields with them, we have to raise frequency etherically to see or feel them. My first experience with the male being I described from last night was when I walked down the stairs of my Zoliart studio towards the mudroom. Halfway down the darkened stairway, I felt the presence of someone behind me. I sat down on the stairs and felt palatable fear. This was around 2016, by the way. I was so terrified that I jumped up, ran down the stairs, and fearfully looked back to see a kindly male being sitting next to where I'd been.

He said, "Hello."

I said nothing. I was terrified. I couldn't speak.

"It's nice here, don't you think?" he continued, smiling. I recall this as the first full-on etheric manifestation from him. More to come later! I still recall the fear. Since then, I have worked on it and am able to detach a bit with humor. The second time I saw him was in my office downstairs, which is now the little museum Cabinet of Curiosities. It was night time and I'd gone in to retrieve something from the closet. My eyes moved to a barely perceivable form sitting on the window seat. I was startled to see a very physical dude smiling, holding a small staff in his right hand.

"Okay," I said as I started to leave. "I'm out of here."

He asked. "Where are you going? Stay a bit."

Oh, no way. I was frozen in the fear mode preceding flight. I managed to stand there for a few seconds before sliding sideways out the door to presumed safety. He meant no harm and surely found my terror amusing. Big psychic researcher! I recall that second encounter a few months after the stair incident. And yes, I'm now more used to seeing entities walk around my home. It is second nature now. It takes me a while to attune to it, maybe a few minutes and then I'm fine. We converse sometimes, but usually, I just observe them going in and out of the several portals in our home.

Several days after the dude sauntered into our bedroom to give me that other meditation, I heard, "You can call him Edward." They'd given me silly names I could call him, all of which I rejected. Sometimes, they like to mess with me.

"No, I want the name he presents and connects with," I demanded. Demands rarely do any good, but I thought I'd try. When I hear these things, it is not an external or even an internal auditory reception. I see the words and know them as though they were speaking to me in my head, seeing them projected on a screen inside my head.

The visuals always accompany the hearing piece. Let me tell you about an event which occurred the day following our three-month spiritual push. I've addressed this period called the spiritual push in other writings, but will give you some bullet points for clarification. The full moon in Aries, which is Easter, is the festival of the Christ. The full moon in Taurus in May is the Wesak Festival, and the full moon in Gemini in June is the Festival of Humanity.

The calendar period from March 20th to June 20th finds hierarchy setting intention and pushing spiritual development. The full moon in June this year was June 3rd 2023. On the 4th of June, I was told by a space brother that they had a setback, a crisis of sorts, because the lords of materiality, the evil dudes, released huge pockets of negativity and hate into the astral realm above certain areas of the planet. Sensitive people channel that down.

This affects humanity to stay stuck and not want to move forward. All sorts of negative emotions are attached to this. Maitreya says that the past is evil. When we are stuck in it, we cannot find God. God is future movement. I don't know what will come of this small setback, but it appears that evil was clever enough to wait until the hierarchy period ended to release their nasty imprints. Our addictions and emotions glam onto these sticky pieces.

The space brother then told me, "We will work through this, but it will take a bit of time. Stay positive."

Love is the only solution, the only road forward, and the single most potent accent we can create. I have been trained painfully, slowly, and not always successfully to observe myself being myself. I write my impressions of my being me. The intuitive hints can be lost if I emotionally rest in ego instead of being responsive to higher power. Here's another example of how I employ a variety of cards, runes, and other tools to discern messages from my own subconscious mind.

The subconscious is our connection to our soul, then to God. It is perfect and knows 100 percent about us in this life as well as hold the records of other incarnations. The hidden subconscious reveals its wisdom when we pray, meditate and allow that feeling nature to speak through the heart. Its language can present in words, images, auditory or tactile phenomena and ways of making itself known to our very busy conscious mind. Several evenings ago, I did a drawing using the archetype cards.

The archetypes are thoughts and structures, the building blocks of human experience. New archetypes present with social and transformative changes in human life. Carl Jung and many other people write and speak on the archetypes and their importance. The card I drew after closing my eyes and asking where am I currently on my journey was the Fault Line. This archetype addresses the nature of disruptive, if not always unpleasant, change.

It's a period of straddling a formerly secure footing split in two, of placing each foot now shaking as it straddles both past and future over the chasm. Last night, I drew the exact same card twice in a row. This happens a lot with me. I closed my eyes and entered an awake-sleep state to search visuals as the fault line archetype presented what is in this chasm. I asked and heard, "It's not what's hiding in there, Zoli, but what is obvious."

"The fault line itself is the focus, not what hides in the chasm. Look at what's in front of your face." Indeed, I am challenged these days with letting go of old, worn patterns, of straddling the crack, unsure of what is next. But I observe both feet firmly on the surface once I am honoring old lessons while trusting that the placement of that other foot is grace. I see the fault line as it cracks open, regaining sure footing with patience. This thing about

Very Capricornian, this thing about time. That whole process of experiencing the fault line is exactly what I require for the mystery of my next step to be revealed. After I draw one type of card or rune, I often consult a different one for an energetic confirmation. I liken this to consulting several teachers of differing opinions. I drew the rune Thurisaz reversed, which looks like a thorn. Thurisaz certainly addressed my fault line card, counseling a quickening of my abilities and lessons, an accelerated period to address the thorny issue.

We're still in the three-month spiritual push period, just between the full moon in Taurus and the third full moon period in Gemini. This rune counsels me to review the learnings I am now leaving behind to maintain a positive state of mind. The reversed Thurisaz suggests I contemplate and reflect on a Taurean theme of what I value in this world. What do I believe? What is my value system? I see reversed runes or cards as similar to the retrogrades in astrology. Retrogrades slow down the action and request a reflective review of issues. It warns against rushing into an uncertain future without adequate respect of what has just occurred.

zoliartexoticamontana.com/music
"Echoes of the Mesa with lyrics"

Your Questions Answered: What is a karmic debt?

Here's a rarely asked question, but one which came to me as I watched one of the wonderful paranormal TV shows I so enjoy. When a discarnate entity, a ghost, causes harm to the living, is there a karmic debt owed? Spirit says yes, absolutely there is, when I asked him about it.

"When interactions present into this physical world, karmic debt accumulates."

I thought on that for a bit, actually surprised at Spirit's answer. I asked. "So how does the dead person repay that debt?"

They said, "Whenever a soul enters into life on Earth for the very first time, he must complete the cycle to the end, even if he takes a million years off in other planetary systems or realities to do so. Some choose birth on other planetary systems or perhaps remain in the higher than physical Earth, that is the astral. But finish, we all must. Each soul is a potential god. Life on Earth requires accountability; the lords of karma control this. You must complete all incarnations on Earth. No matter how many lives you spend elsewhere, you have to return here."

I asked. "What about the mentally ill who hurt others due to their illness."

"The same." They said, "The lords of karma are the accountants. All is accounted for but not in your Earthly terms or in Hammurabi's code. An eye for an eye and a tooth for a tooth so to speak."

"So," I continued. "These debts can be spread out over lifetimes when the conditions are there to repay."

"Something like that," they said. "This is not explicable in Earthly terms; just trust us on this."

At 9:30 at night back in April, I sat in my chair perusing a memento mori skull on Etsy. I like looking at them, and I collect them. And then I psychically heard, "Hi, I'm Peter Robinson," as I was ordering a vampire skull. I quickly searched on Safari for the name Peter Robinson and was intrigued to see Peter Robinson was a British suspense novelist.

It said that Peter was an immensely talented writer over a very wide range of subjects. He wrote short stories, and he wrote poetry. He died his body in 1922. I said hello to this person and thanked him for visiting. I guess he came in to say hello. They do, at times, pique my curiosity at what may have attracted this particular spirit to my being. There is a magnetic, electrical energy which attracts us to each other. Perhaps it is a connection from other lifetimes or states of consciousness.

But then again, it could have been a bunch of BS. I never know.

Chapter 4:
Hidden in Plain Sight

Here is an example of a hidden in plain sight hint from my own life. I often wonder which of the Space Brothers I work with in my specific field. Much delusion and falsehood surround the subject of who one is and where one is from. Benjamin Creme addressed this issue by offering facts about who they really are and why they are here. The other off-worlder beings who have visited and worked here for millennia, are very busy people. They do not pay casual visits, nor do they respond to our beck and call, our curiosity.

If they show up in a lowered frequency and physically formed or ethereally project into our space, there is a valuable lesson for us to discern. There is a reason why they are here. I've written about the Billy event in other books, but I will address it again to clarify my recent understanding of what transpired in 2017. My Zoliart employee and I were in the kitchen of my home here in Montana. She and I both intuited a presence. I then ethereally saw a man standing at the counter.

He was about 5 foot 8, dark, short hair, medium toned skin, dressed in a black close fitting pant outfit and jacket. And he had a logo of a triangle elongated and sideways, accompanying an undecidable script on his left lapel. I was quite taken aback and stared at the smiling form two feet from my face. He gave off a kind but hugely powerful energy. I said, "Well, hey, who the heck are you? Welcome."

He replied, "I'm just here watching you live your life."

I felt like a zoo animal, truly observed and studied, but not in a threatening way. He stuck around for about an hour, staying in place, smiling, watching me at my work, standing at the eating bar he was, one elbow leaning up upon it. I recall a sense of urgency in my desire to know more about him. He said that he would come in time. I began to feel a familiar familiarity, a family feeling around him. He said, "My name is Billy. I am from the high-frequency portal of Mars."

> *When I attune to my intuition and ask what is going on, I'm always surprised at the visuals accompanying the response.*

What was a Martian, clearly a military dude, doing in my kitchen? I then felt a shift in the energy, like an engine revving up. A kind of sparkle enveloped me. I glanced into the kitchen window and saw his image etched into the glass. I grabbed my phone and recorded his picture.

I still have it. I then heard, "I'm Billy. Will-I-Am. William." Bingo! I got it. I recall that Mars is three million years ahead of Earth. They have not made the same stupid decisions that we have made, the same mistakes, and they are two quite distinct populations in the etheric aspect of Mars.

Billy is of the evolved group who will teach Earth the Martian lessons of using our willpower. The age of Capricorn, about 2,000 years from now, will embody this willpower, this aspect of evolution. So, Will I Am, Billy was the hint for me. The lower-level Martians are just a bit above the Earth people. They fight, destroy, compete and revel in the lower frequencies. When Billy left, I felt a sense of urgency again to pull him back, but I couldn't, and I didn't, and I had no reason to.

I'll never forget his visit. He felt like a brother. I felt like I had known him in other times. I was honored.

When I attune to my intuition and ask what is going on, I'm always surprised at the visuals accompanying the response. I can never predict what I'll see. Here's an example. As I drove down the mountain this morning, enjoying the sparkles gleaming off of the Clark Fork River below, I came to the huge rock face connecting our drive to the main road. I always pause a bit here and bless the huge fortress, seeing faces and critters different each time.

Today, I saw a wide wave of sorts rising from the road all the way to the top of the rock face. It was blue in color. I then saw the wave come back down to go under the road and wind down the mountain into the river 300 feet below. The circular pattern continued. I'd never seen this before. Do you see what I mean when I say that surprises always accompany my psychic events? When I do walk-throughs in houses, I'm always surprised by who and what I see show up.

It's quite amazing. Unfortunately, it's always the darned basement. This should make you laugh a bit. Do you wonder if the communication between my guidance and me is always light, love and sweetness? Heck no. Just today, while pondering how I was doing with an irritating situation, guidance responded immediately with, "You're doing better than you think, zip it." Clearly, my irascibility was leaking out of my mouth.

Into a world gone mad, we invoke the light from the heart of God, we invoke the love within and may the light and love manifest and the power to join in one heart and one mind for peace profound.

Create the love we seek. Come all to the festival of light.

zoliartexoticamontana.com/music
"Here Today Gone Tomorrow"

Your Questions Answered: Why are the matters of the paranormal hidden in plain sight?

What isn't? Everything really is. It's no different than anything else, but paranormal is about a different frequency than the five physical senses. We come here with the agreement that the five physical senses will run our lives. And if they don't, you'll end up in a psych ward because you can't tell the difference between what's real and what isn't. So, we have to have the kindness of agreement that if I touch that, it's going to be hot.

The five physical senses are the agreement, but the paranormal world is everything outside of that. In this kind of work, we like to say that the percentage of the five physical senses is the last five minutes on the clock. The other fifty-five minutes is what's really out there. It's everything else. And it's constantly moving, constantly changing.

What's weird about the physical world is that it looks solid. And I have a colleague who says the world really is a matrix. Well, it is, and it isn't. You know, if you look at it from that perspective, it's a perspective. And that gets into our prejudicial beliefs that things are a certain way. We'll get on a kick and say, "No, no, no, this is how it is."

And somebody else says, "No, no, no, it's like this."

But they're all true in a certain way. Let me back up. Angels, for example. Most people believe they see angels, they hear angels, angels can talk to people. Actually, they cannot. Your guardian angel never has a conversation with you. It is the silent voice you don't communicate with. It just keeps you on track. The angelic beings are non-physical beings who have no contact with humanity. Angelology became a thing only in the 1100s AD with the Catholic church. Up to that time, nobody really mentioned angels.

What you see with wings is usually a Master or a Deva that appears as an angel because that's what you believe. You are loved that much. The angelic world is real. The seraphim angels, archangel Michael, all of those beings are real. And they do show up occasionally if they are sent by God. But when people say, well, I'm communicating with the angels, they're not. I'll tell you a quick story.

This is very interesting. There is a gal I contacted maybe ten years ago. I was having some difficulty because I had gotten an energetic attachment. It was demonic attachment, and I was getting sick. So, I found her on the internet, and she did a clearing and this and that. And I don't know if it was real, what she did or not. We started doing a little research together. Once a week, she'd call and she'd do some energy clearing, and she was good at what she did.

Then, one day, this person says that she is a seraphim angel. I immediately thought, now I'm going to discount everything else she said. She had written a book that was unbelievably magnificent, a story about a human being who was actually an angel who came to save the Earth. Well, guess who she said she was.

I immediately went into my kind of research analyst self, and I started asking her about her childhood. Well, her mother was paranoid schizophrenic and would hold her down on the bed and scream at her. So, this woman learned to dissociate. She was not in good health. She drank a lot. She smoked a lot, like a massive amount of humanity does. So, she woke up, and there were these six beings standing in her room. Now, that does happen. But they told her that they were seraphim angel and guess what, so was she. This poor woman was in the presence of some beings from the astral realm who thought they were seraphim angels themselves.

This is what the astral realm is. So, they convinced her that she had all this responsibility, and I think the lady had demonic attachments. I found her very interesting because I'm used to dealing with wackos. She said she was going to come visit for a weekend. I thought she'd never come here because she knows I see her.

I wasn't unkind, but she called, and she said, "You know, I think I'm sick."

I said, Actually, "I think you might be kind of psychotic."

Well, she lost her shit, screamed and yelled, and sent back some presents I sent her. And, of course, went off the chart. That is the best example I have of how you can be deceived by the other side. Now, why was she so attractive to these astral beings? I think she had an agreement with them that she would do this work. She was a gifted writer, I mean, no names mentioned, but this person was just out there.

When people scream and yell, they show their true selves. If she was real, she would have said, "You know, I've wondered about that myself." And then provide a reasonable explanation. But no, she had a commune at her house where other, she called them *angel incarnates*, lived. There, she convinced other people who also wanted to be famous that they were angels too. The world is filled with this stuff. So that's the best example I can give of how insidious this is and how easy it is to be deceived.

It's fascinating because if entities are in your room and they're telling you something, you're inclined to believe them, but you don't realize that they may not necessarily have your best interest. Or be telling the truth.

It's a sticky wicket there. If entities appear in my room, I'm like, what the fuck are you doing? I was asleep. Because the ones that deal with me are smart Alecs, and they're fun. They're like me, but we attract to us only what we are. If you are a good person, you're not going to attract demonic stuff. It can come your way, and you can get attached by it, if you have imprints in you where you've had a curse or something. That's a whole different subject.

But everything that happens to us happens because of attraction and repulsion. That's called the law of attraction. And that is quite real. Now, here's what's interesting. Last month, I was reading a theosophical book by the Master about thought.

So, the statement was, "Thoughts do become real." Everything you think seeks to become real. But my joke about that from years ago when people would say that, and I said they were full of it because they thought they could say anything because it was going to happen. I'd say I could sing "I wish I were an Oscar Meyer Weiner" ten times, and I'm not going to turn into a bratwurst. So come on, people.

Here's the truth about that. If you think something, the thought will circle back around, and it'll go, do you want this? Do you want this? Are you sure you want this? Do you want this? Do you want that? What I have learned to do is if I'm thinking something and it comes up again, I go, nope, I don't want that. Nope. It's not me. Shouldn't have thought that. So, thought does create itself. And it's magnetic. But luckily, I think most people in the developed world are not going to think a bunch of awful, stupid stuff because it makes them feel bad.

And it circles back around. We get obsessed with the thoughts, and usually, we'll go, nope. I don't want that.

Chapter 5:
The Off-Worlder Populations; Aliens

Fear is the great awakener. We humans are just dumb. We're afraid of the wrong things. Most folks react to seeing these guys and their lightships with fear of the unknown. Aliens. The correct response is to say thank you. Thank you for cleaning up our critical mass of pollution in our atmosphere in accordance with what is allowed through karmic agreements. Thank you for your kindness. We will have to repay this grace someday, but now we suffer under the effects of our human low-level choices. These off-worlder beings, our space brothers, are all love.

We are not. There lies the fear. They have always been here, but since the 1930s, their presence and participation in the tragedies have increased because of the nuclear mess. Most is done under an agreement between the abductee and the space brothers. The conscious mind rarely recalls this agreement that it was made on the soul level. There is the fear, the great awakener. Our planetary atmosphere is the skin which separates us from the immediate solar system and universe.

However, here's the dichotomy. There are two distinct populations of humans who experience contact with the space brothers or off-worlders. Agreements from the soul level are usually unconscious and not recalled. Many people have agreed to allow space brothers to harvest their eggs or sperm to improve the off-world races. Most of these humans have connections with the harvesters from other times and perhaps levels on those planets. These are usually non-traumatic encounters.

I have a conscious recollection that I know I have children that are out in space. Keilor, Chelsa, and Dendera. The fourth one, Aurelia, died. These beings must stay out of the gravitational field of Earth. They are only partially human. The second population are from whom the Space Brothers label bio-mass. These are the people who have no connection or commitment to a spiritual path. They are fair game. They are what you might call the nons. What about your abductions occurring by people all over the world? Who is doing this, and why? Let's consider the causes of this rather than reacting to the effect.

> *Abductions are allowed for humans who are not decidedly on a religious or spiritual path.*

So-called abductions are usually real. Some are fake, as with anything else. Abductions are so-called allowed for humans who are not decidedly on a religious or spiritual path. These people lack the mark on their forehead, visible only to the unseen world. A mark, absolutely, it's really there.

The mark is between the eyebrows a little above. The space brothers and spirit say that this is real. These people are labeled this biomass fair game. But how fair is that you ask the ancient practices of baptism, consecration, confirmation, and dedicating a path to, anything higher than your own ego? These are enlightened protection packages, insurance of sorts which marks the human as a possession of God, not anything else.

These are not biomass; it is simply a choice. What do you think about that? There is truly a real visible light on the mark of the forehead visible to other beings. The third eye, the Ajna center, separates this population from the biomass. Can this be true? It is indeed quite so. It is interesting to recall several biblical passages referring to the invisible mark of God's presence within the head and heart. Proverbs 7:3 states the seal has to be placed on the forehead. A mark that angels, not man or human eyes, can read, for the destroying angel must see this mark of redemption.

The intelligent mind has seen the sign of the cross of cavalry in the Lord's adopted sons and daughters. In Ezekiel 9:4, God says that the Prophet has to mark all the mourners from Jerusalem with a sign on the forehead. This refers to the Hebrew letter Taw. In Ephesians 1:13 through 14 it states: And you were included in Christ when you heard the message of truth, the gospel of your salvation when you believed you were marked in his will with a seal. The promised Holy Spirit is a deposit guaranteeing our inheritance until the redemption of those who are God's possession to the praise of his glory.

And then there's the little issue with Mr. Icky Satan himself. The Bible says in Revelation that God sealed 144,000 by placing a mark on their forehead, a seal of light. We don't know if that number is correct, but it's a start. Satan does the same thing by placing the mark of the beast

(Revelation 13:15-17) on his followers. He claims them and brands them with the 666.

Without judgment towards one's beliefs or religion, I suggest a good, hard look at our spiritual path and dedication to higher power is more protective than we might think. The letter taw, in Ezekiel's time, was written as a cross with a long arm at two o'clock, the tail at seven o'clock, and the shorter cross arms at eleven o'clock and four o'clock. A tilted cross it is. The modern Taw is quite different. The word Taw translates as a mark.

So, what should we do? Just love. Goodwill is the most accessible form, the lowest level of love. What should you do? Just love. The aspiration to help each other is the highest form of God's love to move beyond human desires and needs, and then there is true altruism that is rare, hard to express, and challenging to maintain because it comes from the soul. The soul's imprint upon the personality is what fuses the love aspect of selfless service to our behavior.

Earth itself is a Ray 2 planet, and the USA is a soul Ray 2 place. Each planet in this solar system expresses under one of the 7 Rays. Ray 2 is the Love Wisdom Ray. The Christ energy is love, and the Buddha energy is wisdom. Both Christ and the Buddha are brothers and work together. This Earth is the only planet in our solar system to produce a Christ. The Masters of Wisdom, those former human beings who achieved enlightenment through meditation and service, began returning into this world in 1975.

One at first. Then, a couple, a bit later. Then 14 Masters were present by 2006. Maitreya entered this world and this scenario in 1977. Love is their signature. Love is all they do. Our love is stimulated by their presence here, affording us the great opportunity of sacrificing the little personality and the will for the greater will and the soul's purpose of serving. I could indeed write pages on this, but I suggest that you research your own work through shareinternational.org writing, as well as the works of Benjamin Creme.

Your Questions Answered: Are humans aliens?

No. They're not, they're people. Here's the confusion in that. When you are born in a human body, you are born of a woman. You're a person, right? You can get on ancestry.com; you can track your DNA. There's proof for that. So, when people run around, and I used to do this, saying I'm an alien, it just means you don't fit in. You haven't figured out who you are yet, but guess what? Your soul may definitely be from somewhere else.

So, in my understanding, most of us on this Earth are from somewhere else in the solar system. We are seeded. It's called being star-seeded. There are beings who are who first took their first breath on the moon. There are beings who, when God created them, took their first breath in the Pleiades. That's very fashionable right now. Everybody wants to be a Pleiadean. Well, you're not, and you can't say it enough to make it be real.

I know what planet I was originally created on, maybe a million years ago. But I'm not an alien. I'm a person. You see what I'm saying? A lot of the times when people say, "Well, I'm an alien in a human body." I think that's what they're saying, but then, a lot of times you're just nuts. You're just not figuring it out and want to be different and get attention. I've known plenty of people like that. Then there's a thing about the walk-ins, and that's also a big one.

You're not a walk-in. Your soul didn't leave, and somebody else came in. If that's true, it may be one in a billion, which means that there are only eight on the planet. I'm just joking about that. You see what I'm saying? I don't think that's real at all. We try to run away from who we are and our karma. And the new age community, that's the most dangerous religion on the planet. It is so dangerous because it's running away from belief systems that may be true or not, but they've created their entire religion and all of the dogma that goes with it. And they will insist that they are right. Oh, all dogmas do that.

There are people, aliens that are walking on this Earth, but they are not human people. They're humans from maybe Mars. I've got a picture of the one that came into my kitchen. In my understanding, what they say about it and Theosophy also agrees with this: When God created the form in his image, beings created in this solar system have a head, two arms, two legs, and a torso. It is called the heavenly man. The cosmos is also set in that pattern. It's laid out to look like that. So, God really did create people in His image.

There are beings from other planets who aren't humanoid-looking, like the Zeta Reticuli. A lot of what you see with the Zeta is their mental projections from other places. There are some that act like computers. What would you call that? They're made of biomass. It's too far beyond me to even understand. Everything you can think of is out there, but it's not necessarily right here.

There are motherships that are the size of the state of Rhode Island. They are huge, and they just travel all over the universe. They are called starships or motherships. There are also smaller ones. There are all kinds of them that you can imagine. The ships that you see in the sky here were made on Mars. In our solar system, they're all made on Mars because they're really good at that.

There are triangular ships. There are cigar-shaped ships. There are round ones. Literally, anything you can imagine is out there. And the fear that's been created around this is just stupid. It's dumb. And humanity has been taught to be afraid. If people knew the kindness, concern and brilliance of the Martians, Venusians and the like, the fear would melt. The Jupiterians also are here to help. The Plutonians don't. They're even below Earth.

They're just evil. I say that in the term that they aren't based on service. They're not even up to the lowest Earth level. But everyone's here in service. They're trying to help us. They're mopping up all the nuclear radiation that we have on the planet. They're mopping up all the crap in the air. There's plastic everywhere. So, I believe we are going to get it, and we're at the point now that the ships are being revealed more, but we're very concerned about not revealing too much.

And I do say we. We're very concerned not to reveal too much because we don't want to scare people. There's not going to be any mass landing on the White House lawn. That's stupid. Why would you do that? That's not loving. Mars is three million years ahead of us. They don't need us. They don't want to scare us. When the Martian Billy was standing in my kitchen, I felt like a lab rat. It was amazing: the energy, the love, the compassion, the intelligence.

I thought this was just magnificent and terrifying. But when people do not have a belief in any sort of higher power, they're called biomass. And they are allowed to be operated on and taken up and had painful things done because these people have no spirituality. They believe they are the ruler of their lives. They think there's nothing bigger than them. They think they're gods. So, you do have a mark on your forehead if you have a belief in higher power, if you've been dedicated. And that mark on the forehead is a light, and that can be seen by etheric beings.

And you want that light. Believe me. You do want that. Because the so-called forces of evil can also see that, and they won't mess with you. They're not allowed to. Everything goes by agreement. Even the nefarious things agreed to this agreement. They are bound by it.

Everything has to have law. That's what's so bizarre about what's happening right now in this country that laws are just thrown out the window. Smash and grab in stores. Hollywood Boulevard—you can't even go there anymore. They tell people don't wear jewelry, don't take a purse because you will be robbed. Law is what controls everything. As above, so below; the laws of above control the laws of below.

And these aren't man-made laws. These are laws of light, love, and power that were set into what is called the plan of light, love, and power for humanity that hierarchy guards and those laws never change. They never change. So even the nasty ones, God will use evil to test people. Think about Job. If God wanted to get rid of evil, God would get rid of evil. But then, how the heck will we learn anything?

You can't just live at Baskin Robbins or something, you know. And we're just so dumb. We really are. We don't learn unless something gets our attention. Once you get into the level of Mars or, you know, going to the planet Sirius, which is incredible, you evolve so fast there. None of this negative stuff is there because you know who you are. You know that you are a part of God.

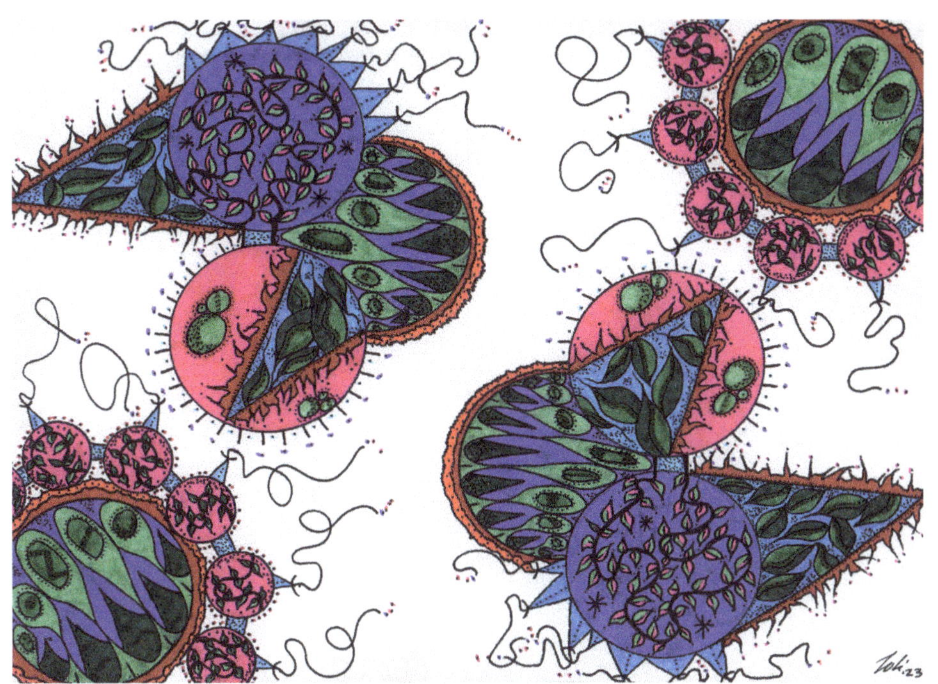

Chapter 6:
Evil 101

You know the feeling. You walk into a room, and something feels off. You try to ignore it because you don't want to out your fears to everybody else. You assume they aren't picking up on the same icky feeling. You calm yourself and search the room for anyone or anything that could explain why you're weirded out. Nothing. Everybody else looks normal. Everything seems okay. No serial killers behind the bar. So, you take a breath and forget about it.

Who hasn't experienced something like this? Your spider senses are your first alarm. Your PSD, your personal security detail's first circle alert that something isn't right. Why do we try to talk ourselves out of these moments of absolute clarity? Usually, this is because the five physical senses aren't what's required to detect supernatural signatures. What, then, are we sensing? If the five senses detect nothing, isn't everything okay? Nope.

Our five inner senses, though, are running all the time. They're running interference for the external ones incapable of speaking spider sense lingo. You know what you feel, right? But how can we train ourselves to recognize this inner security detail? In demonology, we say whoever controls the neurotransmitters controls the mind and, therefore, controls the body. The demonic and icky ones that have nothing better to do than cause disruption have no form.

They want a physical body to experience Earthly delights. Oft times, those delights include feeding off the pain they cause human beings. Demons have no form. They depend on this material world to manifest. Most of their false power comes from riding on ours. Everything is alive in its own world, but not everything speaks the language you understand. The Lords of Materiality's real job, the forces of evil that is, is to hold in place physical matter. I know you're wondering what that means. Is she dismissing the emotional aspect of the icky ones? Nope. Look at it this way. God allows evil to overstep its bounds because we have free will. Millennia ago, we overstepped ours. We chose desire, comfort, all the seven deadly sins and their relatives over waiting for God's time to fill in the spaces. Those spaces are the test we endure in silent moments prior to screwing up.

We are an impatient lot addicted to wanting our way right now. When we don't get it, we open Pandora's box to see what she left us to force God's hand. The contents of that box live in our emotional desire body. It hurts not to indulge in that addiction when we imagine we can get away with it, just this once, yep, one time, okay? But the original job description of evil was to hold matter in place, to assure that when I look at a chair it will still look like a chair when I turn around a minute later. You had one job, evil...

They overstepped this job description during the Atlantean period, hundreds of thousands of years ago. The war between good and evil ended in a tie. The demonic were left on the Earth, while the Masters of Wisdom, Hierarchy, retreated to the mountain ranges of Earth to await the time when their words could be heard. That time is now. About 60 Masters are now on the Earth in the etheric and physical etheric bodies. More on that later, I promise.

It's a really complex subject, but I will address it in another writing. So, why do we folks do awful things? Why do the seven deadly sins ride our emotions like a banshee on holiday? During the Atlantean era, people were just learning what emotions are and how to use them. Up to that time, the race had learned only how to control the physical body during the period of Lemuria much earlier. So, emotion was new and weird.

Most people could not think well and were ignorant of the connection they had to the soul. But a handful of the more evolved, led by Lucifer from Saturn, became greedy and evil controllers of everybody else. Lucifer dropped his magnificent cloak of light and fell into the sensual attractiveness of the lower three chakras, the emotions connecting one to believe that all material things are more important than God's world. Lucifer had previously entered the incarnational cycle of Earth. We all have to finish what we started, even Avatars. Yes, he was an Avatar who was sent here to help. Boy, did he ever mess up his mission!

> *Lucifer dropped his magnificent cloak of light and fell into the sensual attractiveness of the lower three chakras, the emotions connecting one to believe that all material things are more important than God's world.*

He was called here to teach the development of Capricornian gifts, including invention, using matter to create beauty and things of the world. Lucifer was a Master of this plane and fit very well into it until he became obsessed with feeding his addictions. Notice how this happens with people, too. Take a look around. We are all one choice away from that decision.

But back to Lucifer. After many incarnations, his personality forgot God and became evil. In December of 1944, he was sent back to Saturn after the Allied forces won over the evil satanic Hitlerian axis energy. Hitler channeled Satan. He was a truly evil personality, a very gifted medium. And the German people were and are very mediumistic. It didn't make them bad. They were just overwhelmed, literally. Hitler was overshadowed by the satanic energy during his explosive speeches.

He was a truly evil soul and is now in a special place, so to speak. Well, if that stuff doesn't get your panties in a wad, I don't know what would. Gives me the heebie-jeebies every time I think about it. I'm sure you're wondering why Satan, who lost the right to be called Lucifer, is on Saturn. And why is evil still so prevalent on Earth? Earth is the home of more beings dedicated to continuing Satan's plan of destroying humanity.

They hate us. They hate love. All they give is pain. They have no free will. They have no physical bodies. They are miserable. That's it. Evil is here and able to work because guess who is addicted to emotion? People. We are still emotionally in that Atlantean period. Emotion runs over logic, love, and feeling. The whole mess of it destroys detachment. Desolation wins over consolation, pure and simple. So how do we fix that? How do we detach from the deadly sins, the emotional fears, hates, distrust and drama? We can learn love.

Glory Be to the Father, and to the Son, and to the Holy Spirit.
As it was in the beginning, is now, and ever shall be, world
without end.

We can learn meditation and service. Those two things lead us to God: no matter what religion you are, no matter what path. If we raise our emotions and focus on that sixth chakra, called the Ajna center, that colors the emotions, right in between your eyebrows is where it lives. Emotion lives in the third chakra. They never reach the fourth, which is the heart. Most people live with the first three chakras: sexuality, pain, and fear. But guess what? If we focus on that area between the eyebrows, the sixth chakra will pull that energy up to the heart.

And that is calming. Try it. It takes practice. That's why we call it a spiritual practice. Where is hell? What do we call the hellish realm? What we call the hellish realm are actually levels one and two of the astral realms. And what the heck is that? We pass our days on Earth clothed in fleshy bodies, but we are surrounded with several other bodies made of finer material. One of them is the astral body. It's our emotional body. There are several levels to the astral realm.

It's where we go when we die in this body, what we call heaven, hell, and purgatory. Picture a fine mist surrounding your body. This is our astral body. When we leave our bodies at night to fly through the dream worlds, we transfer our consciousness into the astral body. Where does it go? Sometimes, we bring these memories back into consciousness, but sometimes we don't. So, which is which? What we call hell, the lower first and second levels, are actually real. That first lower astral level is what we call hell. It is woven into the fiber of Earthly life because it falls between the Earth's surface and a bit below. Maybe this is why we can be so affected with addictions. It's kind of walking around with us. Even Pope Francis says that God never condemns anyone to what they think is hell. Your own desolation sends you there. If you believe it, you do that all by yourself.

Level one is a little bit below the Earth. That's why we identify hell as below us. Level two is a bit above the ground which explains why ghosts seem to partially float. The first two levels are icky. And remember that emotions lead us to any and all astral levels. Isn't it great to practice positive thinking? The more conscious we become, the more aware we become of how we can control our emotions with love, and the higher we go after many lifetimes of evolving.

Can you see how easy it is for us emotional humans to feel the icky stuff in our faces from these two lower levels? We swim in it, literally. Evil beings shoot fear, pain, and crazy ideas into the astral realm, and we channel them down.

Channeling, what is that? It's an aspect of only the emotional body, the third chakra. All channeled information comes from the third chakra area. The higher beings and higher writings are called *mediated*.

They come from the heart, the fifth and the sixth levels. But channeling isn't all bad. There is much beauty and truth there, but it's just emotional. We also channel a bunch of garbage and call it true. We channel one abstract ideal, imagining it is true, and then create dictatorships espousing its validity. We're kind of nuts in that way. Astral levels 3 and 4 are what we call heaven. We go there and wait for orders. We meet with beings that have died before who are still there.

But sometimes, if we expect to see Aunt Sarah, and she died a really long time ago, another being out of love will appear and look just like her. That is how much we are loved. There's so much to say about the astral realm and what it really is. But a lot has been written on that, so I'm not going to delve too deeply into it. Whatever you believe is yours. Astral levels 5 through 7 are magnificent indeed.

There, you would find choirs of angels, the Christ, the Avatar, the great beings who communicate with us through those levels. But many magnificent books are channeled through the lower levels, like *A Course in Miracles*, channeled from a disciple of the Master Jesus. So, there you have it, Evil 101. Chew on this a while and maybe search for more information on Theosophy, or maybe search out the name Maitreya.

Once again, I don't have all the answers, but you already know that. Oh, how we love so deeply and fully all those and that which reminds us of ourselves. The valued similarities are the familiar ring of the tones comprising the songs of similar souls. Oh, how we love the reflection of our own stories, so similar, so consistent, so comforting with what we find in others. But here is the lie and the truth. We are but one soul, one human soul, one family of humanity shining on countless stars throughout the universe.

The story of countless lives birthing stories of oh so many ways of being! We love to continue these stories, praying and hoping that they will never end and never die. But death in the physical form is the law. We extend our feelings, our soul's purpose, in the times we have left. And we love. Love is the answer.

zoliartexoticamontana.com/music
"Lay Me Down"

Your Questions Answered: What's the difference between demons and the paranormal?

Well, they are actually two different things. The paranormal covers anything that is outside the five physical senses. Para means around like parapsychology, and it's taken on the meaning of just being woo-woo. And it depends on what age you're in. They didn't use that term back in the eighteen hundreds when Blavatsky and the Fox sisters were going, and all the mediumship was happening. I don't know what they called it.

Paranormal covers anything that's not the five physical senses. It's around the normal. And I really think that what we call normal is what we can attend to with our five physical senses. Paranormal is anything that we can't explain in that way.

The demonic is part of the paranormal. I differentiate between demons and daemons. The Greek interpretation of daemons was these were beings that helped humanity.

They were neither good nor bad. They were neutral. They're hugely powerful. And what they do is they speak in higher terms to us, and they translate from us to the higher beings. They're messengers, so to speak. And, of course, in the world of fanatical religions or whatever, anything that's like that is bad. But that group would also include the Olympic spirits. One of them is Aratron. I've done a lot of work with him. I have a story in *The Reality Pirate's Journal* about an experience I had at the farm that I will share again because it addresses that.

There is a place down in the lower pasture. It's a very wooded, beautiful area called Beaver Creek, and there are beavers in there. And I would sit on that little wooden bridge and ponder things, talk about things. Every now and then, I would just do a meditation, or I'd do a shamanic journey. And I was doing that one day, and I was just felt I was in an altered state, and I was sitting down on the bridge with my feet hanging over with my head down. I felt a presence to the right, I looked up, and I was looking at a pair of tall black boots.

And the being in the boots said, "Come with me." And so, I did. I didn't physically go. This was in one of the other bodies. I did go with him and I went way back into the woods into the forest. There are ten acres of forest in that area of beautiful cedar trees with ferns on the floor. It's a very moist, temperate rainforest area. And I saw the whole hillside open up. And there were all of these dwarves working along there. And I said, "So this is where you are."

I had been working with some dwarves, but I had no idea how to find them. I have looked for who these guys are. They're about two to three feet tall at the most. They are unclothed. They have feet, kind of like a hobbit. They're a little big. And they look like a human dwarf so to speak, but they never have clothes on, and they are silent. And I had been seeing in my mind's eye and working with one named Lily, and then I met another one.

His name was Durga, and he took me to see where they lived and worked inside the Earth. That was amazing to me. Then, I immediately popped back into my body, I guess sitting on the bridge, and I heard, "My name is Aratron." And I thought, well, it must be an alien. I went in the house and looked it up in my psychic books. And I found that Aratron was an Olympic spirit.

What he does is he gives you helpers. So, as part of my job, I have always worked with things that other people are scared of. The gnomes, the little fire beings, the gargoyles, the trolls, all these little guys that are just maligned so to speak. That is an example of a demon that can be interpreted as demonic or angelic. It's really hard to define what that is.

On the other hand, if you talk about true demons, they have no physical form at all. They have nobody. They have no physical form, but they have been given certain forms by human imagination. So, they can take those on, and they do appear a certain way. There are demonic beings that you can work with who are not bad, but they're still demonic. It's very strange, and it doesn't match any of the religions. And if people don't know what they're doing and they mess with that, it's like walking down in a bad part of town in the middle of the night. You see what I'm saying? You can't define everything as far as good and bad.

Good and evil live in the same cup. And when we fill that cup with water, they swirl around. We can't tell what's what. And that's what life is. Our job is to discern that and find how to do that. So how do you do it? It's hard. The religions are one way. The spiritual paths are one way. The Heart Math Institute is another way. There are all kinds of ways that teach us the good way of being.

I saw that, and I thought, well, that's the most irritating thing there is because we want to know. And we project onto others. We do it in life all the time. We project on to other people what we're trying to get. We say they're doing it so that we don't have to see ourselves doing it. And part of the ownership of authenticity is to catch those projections.

Chapter 7:
Facing Fear of the Icky Stuff

Demonic beings hate mirrors. If they see the image of the physical form they have temporarily inhabited, they will withdraw in pain and repulsion from seeing themselves as they truly are. I often have asked why my homes are resplendent with mirrors of all shapes and sizes. Maybe that explains it. I myself am simply too old to look at them and smile. Christ's work enters that if he offers his soul as requested, the attacks will stop. He said, that I have told you this while I am with you.

The advocate, the Holy Spirit, who the Father will send in my name, will teach you everything and remind you of all I have told you. The demonic received neither promise nor grace from the advocate. They have a collective will but no free will. The demonic hierarchy seethes with hate for men's free will. Never ever play with Ouija boards, by the way.

A demonic entity called Zozo is attached to it and could quite easily manipulate it when two people join forces to call on the unknown.

Just as Jesus promised to be there when two or more of us are together and gathered in my name, so does the demonic mimic that, putrefying the promise by invoking the opposite. When two or more of us invoke unknown beings, always true with the Ouija board, the demonic has invited permission to appear. Dark beings with malintent are capable of opening portals. When we sense, feel, and encounter beings, we enter into a shared space with them. We are in their world as they are in ours.

Indeed, this holds true for the benevolent ones also. Because satanic beings are purely spiritual, and they have no body, no soul, they are enraged that we have both. They cannot take a soul unless someone offers it to them. This can and does happen when a satanic worshiper offers it, but it can also happen if someone who is under attack believes that if he offers his soul as requested that the attacks will stop. We need to develop and practice strength and courage.

These evil forces prey on low-hanging fruit because they are lazy. Be strong and know you are never alone. When obsessions and possessions occur, they are cyclical.

These evil forces prey on low-hanging fruit because they are lazy. Be strong and know you are never alone. When obsessions and possessions occur, they are cyclical. True possession is very real. It is also very rare. The entities retreat, and they will re-enter in cycles. Know this. Oft times, the evil formless spirits appear as inhuman or demonic in appearance. They do this for several reasons, including the fact that they are more associated with the lower animal nature than humanity is, and that they, being formless, cannot fully copy the facial features of a soul inhabited human.

That's interesting, isn't it? When we observe inhuman appearances or inhuman behaviors, it goes against our right reaction to what is good and decent. The evil forces use those things to create the fear response they feed on. During a cleansing or an exorcism, the affected might vomit peculiar objects, foul-smelling fluids or black goo. The objects are actually not in their stomach, but they are manifested in the mouths of demonic beings. These objects and fluids are material manifestations representing the awfulness of the demonic.

Let's discuss greed for a minute. Greed is one of our deadly sins that we can define as a selfish want, a desire to possess for oneself what the body demands for satiation of its wants. Greed is not just for the rich.

Other people's possessions, the material eye candies viewed online and in stores, addictive substances including food, all of these personality-based demands are birthed in the emotions and mind's eye. We certainly do need food. It's not an addiction. Overeating is just a compulsion.

We just do it. We don't seem to be able to stop. I am trying to settle an internal argument that rattles around in my thought process like the cold wind on a warm day.

Maybe you have better insight into the conundrum than I do. The irritant is that the subject of personal power is marked as control over other people. Greed lives in our personality and is a sibling to jealousy. Have you heard folks claim how powerful they are because they have so-called manifested things from their thought process?

This, once again, is force, not power. This claims a source of all things to be themselves. Why do we want, and why do we force things?

The competitive personality gloats when we get what we want, but at what expense? The ego rushes to be first as it fears being last; it seeks more and more, bigger, better, unaccountable for everything. Our desire body swims in that pool while God whispers from the shore. There's an ending to everything we do.

All of our actions, possessions, hopes, plans, and all things in the material world have an end. The ray of destruction before regeneration is Ray 1. It is necessary as it removes old forms from regeneration. What is created is new, and it is the old that needs to be destroyed energetically. This is the way of the world. All thoughts and dreams continue actually in the other worlds, but what does it mean to belong to the world? Are we so addicted to satiation of the five physical senses that we forget where we came from? Why do we become enthralled with the sensations, the glamour, the illusions feeding our worldly selves? My own so-called addiction to addiction, which is what I call my brain, feels like a tsunami of emotion threatening every port of my sanity.

My sanity comes from one source: God. When I remember that we are all the same creatures experiencing the phenomena of sanity, overwhelmed by sensations of this world, my life goes great. "The world hated them because they did not belong to the world." John 17:14.

Speaking from personal experience, I certainly created much drama in my early years, turning to the sensations and distractions of the world because I was unsettled, young, and just dumb. At my age of the crone energy now, I find it painful to look back at my own dumb choices and what came of them, but such is life. What we aspire to do must be born in the intuitive knowledge that it is possible or at least a considered probability. Everything is connected.

zoliartexoticamontana.com/music
"Cowboy With Two Souls"

Your Questions Answered: How do we know good from evil?

Well, thank God we're protected. We really are protected. God protects children and fools. But we are definitely protected because when you agree to come to Earth school, you have to stay in the reincarnation cycle till you're done, and it can be millions of years. So, there is a lot of protection. But it depends on what you think protection is. Does protection mean nothing bad should happen? A lot of it is our choice.

How do you know good and evil? Come on. You know the difference. People actually do, and then we choose what is easiest. We choose Satan when God isn't fast enough.

Then there are the people who don't have that conscious or inner voice that tells them when something is wrong. That is psychopathology. It's sick. They're lacking. Not all psychopaths do awful things. They can be very useful. So how do you use them? How do you apply them? Some of them don't want to be like that. But if you have empathy, that's love. That's your heart. And the greatest ability we have is the ability to serve others.

When empathy is not there, sickness happens. God plays dice. There are faults that happen in the human body. There are defects. They don't have that mechanism for feeling. And I've definitely met some people like that. They're very narcissistic in their behavior. They're charming, and some of them are just flat-out evil. Others, they're just dumb. They think they can get away with this, this, and this.

Chapter 8:
Understanding the Seven Deadly Sins

Do we watch crime shows and stories depicting evil in a passive way to determine what we could get away with? The seven deadly sins are implanted in all of us. I jokingly say when we're born, we get a backpack filled with all of them to carry our whole life. It's a great learning tool. We create our own hells and wonder why others aren't in it with us. So, we magnetize to us those sharing our own hell frequency, and so it goes. And I'm here defining hell as the unpleasant, unacknowledged, irritating stuff that we get ourselves into.

Watch the criminals and see how they get away with their evils. Can we manage that? They appear to enjoy wealth, addiction, and apparent happiness, but for how long? We watch, waiting for the other shoe to drop, and when it does, we secretly wonder what we would do in that situation. We watch the consequences unfold, sitting in our jammies, enjoying our homes while watching evil act out in front of us, knowing we can turn it off at any minute from that box in front of our eyes.

We become our nightmares and our joys by enacting the glamours of this world. It all will end. What and who are we when it does? Perhaps the most notable value of my work is just the sheer volume of it. Thank you, autism, for the unbroken focus. Yesterday, my friend Troy asked me how I managed to produce the works. I replied, autism! We can be peculiarly focused in one area and totally incompetent in another. We tend to collect what intrigues us and have problems tracking but focus intently on what we're doing.

I collect ideas, colors, and stories of human experience. My music is storytelling. I'm a balladeer who has never met the subject she writes of and sings about but attunes to the visuals floating in my head from the collective. It's all there. We just have to record it. We receive and process thousands of inputs daily. We must have the neural network of receptors specific to imprint in order to become conscious of the material we are receiving.

The electrical material sent needs to be magnetized to our very being. The signatures of my writing are love and communication, not shock and confusion. I'm always teaching myself, hopefully from kindness and humor, and directing my words to the greater whole rather than the intellectual elite. I identify as a member of the spiritual masses, not using quarter words in a ten-cent conversation. Those small cents are powerful in their simplicity and elegantly present the love I feel for people, for humanity.

I do love and like people. Although I love and adore animals, people are first. Why? We control the care of the animals. I sometimes hear someone say they like animals more than people, and I want to say, "When you look in the mirror, if you don't like people, you don't like yourself. You think you're a unicorn?" We are always the object of our

own displeasure. Love is all there is, folks. There's no end to it. Love is all that survives. I sometimes wonder why anyone would be interested in reading anything I write.

After several minutes of self-judgment and curiosity, I always conclude that we people are a voyeuristic and curious lot. We just want to see ourselves in others and make sure we're okay. Mirror neurons and the desire to be a part of something bigger than ourselves presses us to seek those familiar places in the lives of other people. I like to believe that my authenticity and dislike for pretense are the common denominator brightening the heart of the reader.

And by the way, when I AM inauthentic and when I AM pretentious, the results are not good. I continually ask the reader to check within his or her own heart and mind for the truth, as I can be as flawed as a dropped stitch. I'd like to believe that others find humor in my insecurities, my apparent flaws, as well as my unusual ability to access other realities. The inherent ability to intuit is not equally distributed in this world.

But where I am gifted, you may struggle to experience. But where your flowers bloom, mine may rot. Everything is communicating all of the time in unspoken language. Everything communicates energetically. All material objects, natural organic things, animals, cells, atoms, molecules, everything seeks joining this world through communication. Subtleties rule. Intuitive hints and visuals are the sensory language presenting singular signatures.

The sounds and sights communicate through our transmission and reception of that language. God's world is a busy place. Silence hides the unspoken language until consciousness seeks it out. We recognize things by the shape of their edges. When I see a chair, I recognize it as a chair, and that is communication born from the learned recognition of physical shapes. In my world, when I ask, "What is that?" it communicates its shape and signature through my five physical senses. Our minds search for hints and synchronicities and the thing and ask what could that thing be.

In some sense, I write to let you know that I do not know. My reticence is researching my peculiarities, and I like to question things. Achieving balance and not doing things in a balanced way; is quite different. Balance is an abstract ideal we aspire to achieve by acting in a balanced way. The give and take of polar opposites seek its homeostasis, which is never permanent. As the waves of the sea go in and out, so do we practice staging balance by teetering precariously on the sharp edge of behavior.

I am often reminded to beware of desperation as its energy signature attracts victimhood and loss of access to personal power. We turn to Satan when God's timing is too slow for us. That power comes from our free will. When I practice that signature of fear, peace of mind is replaced by my personality's insatiable desire for immediate gratification in the physical realm. How do we overcome the negativity? This balancing activity ends only with high initiations, which is a scarcity in our global population. We're just not there yet. For me, seeking balance begets imbalance when I can detach from desire, when I can just feel God and just feel balance and the Advocate's presence within, that's balance for me.

The hum of being in the present moment shortens the distance between the opportunity-seeking balance. Why can I not live in that state? Because it's just me being me. Balance is that abstract ideal we aspire to, never totally manifesting it as a permanent state but a hope and a dream of effort.

zoliartexoticamontana.com/music
"Denial on Trial"

Your Questions Answered: Why is there so much greed?

Greed, one of the seven deadly sins, activates when we feel lack, real or delusionally perceived. It is a lower chakra safety mechanism serving the reptilian neurology to protect the self from losing things, losing people, and losing activities. Greed is similar to a vestigial organ. It serves no positive position in the hierarchy of the heart of goodwill, being the lowest form of love. Feelings of goodwill are heartfelt and overwhelm the reptilian brain's reaction to the potential of loss.

Charisms are the gifts, the favors granted to us by God through the Holy Spirit. These abilities allow us to access the great unseen worlds, allowing us the power to channel and mediate, which are the third and sixth chakras, God's will. These gifts come adorned with thorns. Their flowery scented graces cause disruption in the political correctness and dying modes of passing times.

Expect not the lauds and cheers from others, for Christ comes to set the new against the old.

Maitreya, the world teacher, stated that the past is evil, as is separation from others. Moses was an avatar who fell to Earth to demonstrate his co-creation of superhuman events, with God separating the waters. Jesus, as Christ, walked on the surface of the waters of the sea near Capernaum in John 6:16-21. He overcame the emotions; which is the third chakra with love, the fourth chakra, represented by water. Did he really walk on the water? We don't know.

We assume so. But water is emotion. The huge bodies of water are unpredictable and treacherous, uncontrolled by man's fear of its power. When Moses joined with God's power to divide the Red Sea, so did the division manifest to demonstrate how we are challenged to divide our consciousness from the controlling treacherous emotions and the loving calm of the heart and the mind, which is the sixth chakra, the Ajna center. The Hebrews were not strong enough to divide the sea by their own power.

They were not wise enough to lead themselves through the desert for 40 years. The avatar Moses did this for them. When Jesus achieved his fourth-degree initiation and died his body on the cross, the era of powerlessness ended. Blood sacrifice was now done. He demonstrated what we must do to achieve godliness by sacrificing this world and its addictions and its dramas, to detach and align our hearts and minds with God. It doesn't mean to die on the cross, but to die to the ways of the world.

Water from the side of Christ is represented in the Eucharist by the holy water, which the priests add to the wine, the blood of Christ, before the transubstantiation. During the transubstantiation, Christ transmutes the wine and host into the replicated frequency of his blood, water, and body. Ray 7, the age of Aquarius, is symbolized by the water bearer. We are seeing crises in water on this planet and how water moves over the Earth. Ray 7 presages the next 2,500-year cycle of Capricorn.

The fluids of the physical body, the blood, the cerebrospinal fluid, intra- and extracellular fluids of the body are gradually transforming into greater capacity to receive light from God. During Moses' time, during the 2,500-year age of Pisces, the fishes symbolize these energies of regeneration and sacrifice. When Jesus manifested the loaves and the fishes, it represented the body of Christ manifested in Pisces. We were being shown what we are required to denounce in the depths of the darkness of the soul, that silence of deep-sea darkness.

The monasteries, the rules of St. Benedict, and the quest to go within to demonstrate God's hierarchy and eternality, those times prepared us to direct the watery emotions towards deep inner awareness. These present Aquarian energies, the water bearer, and the 2,500-year cycle of Aquarius challenge us to carry those emotional waters as we manifest his works in the world. We can only feel the Aquarian energies in a group, which is three people or more. As he said, where you are in my name together, I am there.

To utilize the Piscean going within lessons and retain our own boundaries of who we are, that is our lesson now. Our individual skills in facing the group honoring the group will require control of the fluid and emotions we make collectively into the group's initiations. In the future, we will move collectively into group initiations. The collective gatherings in His name. We are currently experiencing mass violence, riots, and anger on airplanes, especially, which is the acting out of control violence from the fear base of any of unevolved humanity.

Chapter 9:
Turn the Other Cheek

Who in their right mind would turn the other cheek if someone whacked you on your face? But in Matthew 5:38-42 it says that Jesus suggested just that. Really? But here's the truth. This was demonstrated to us during mass when Father Carver called up a compadre and showed us what the truth was. I about fell off my pew. In those times, as is still true in many cultures, one shakes hands with, touches objects, and eats with the dominant hand, usually the right one.

Bathroom breaks engage the other hand, the left hand, to do, well, you know. Visualize two people facing each other. One whacks the other on the cheek, and their right hand hits the left cheek. If the attackee turns the other cheek, the attacker will have to use his verboten hand to strike him again. Aha! Jesus was telling us to use our own common sense, to disallow a second attack, to be shrewd by turning the other cheek.

He was a wise dude indeed.

Your Questions Answered: Why is vengeance such a powerful force?

Well, because we want to hurt what hurts us. I mean, it's all below the heart. It's this childish thing. It's survival. You see when you're living in survival, it's those first three chakras below the heart: sexuality, pain, and power. That's the first, second, and third chakras, the seals of the body. If you're living in all that as most of the world is, vengeance is going to seem like it's your right. You're right because it's a survival tool.

All people see is injustice, and yet nobody gets away with anything. Sooner or later, it all rolls around. My mom's frequent statement was, "Revenge is often best served cold." By then, we're not so emotional about it. But what she also said about that is, "If it's cold, you probably talked yourself out of it anyway." She was wonderful.

And I'm sitting here thinking about recovery, the twelve steps. I think that the religions and spiritual paths and the twelve step programs, they teach you how to avoid acting on emotional drama. They teach you self-control, and it takes self-control to not be vengeful.

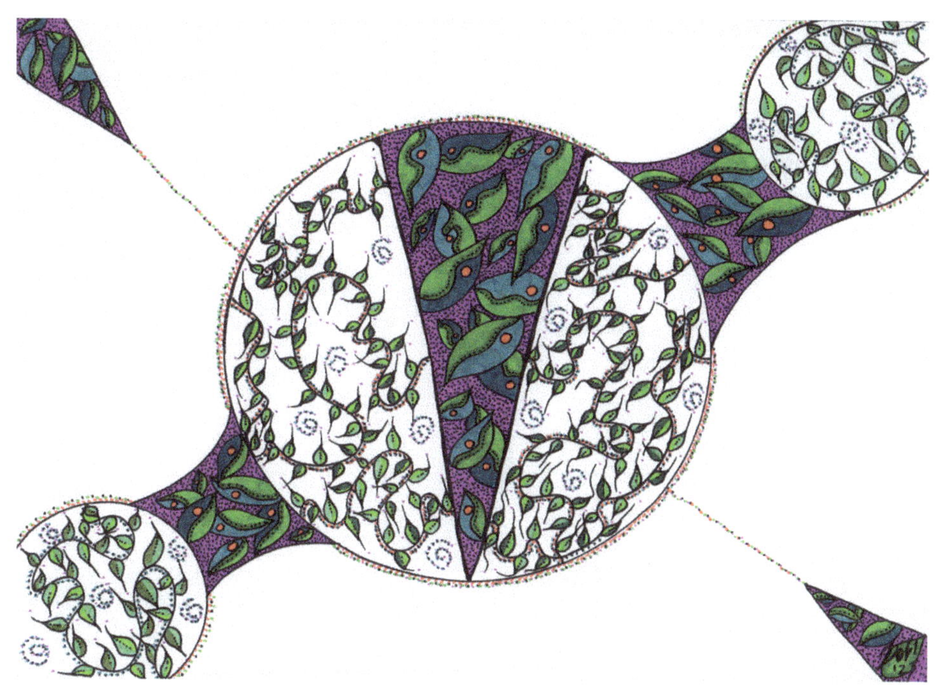

Chapter 10:
Healing Addiction and Recovery

We are a stressed and avoidant society. I myself voted for medical marijuana in both Washington and Montana. It's a miracle drug and a magnificent alternative to some of the heavier drugs. Sometimes. My husband has the correct assessment of this when he says that we need to isolate the beneficial aspects of marijuana into a pill of sorts so that we can titrate it and know exactly what we're getting, how we're getting, and when to take it. How many prescriptions say, "Go home, grow this drug and take as much of it as you want, whenever you want."

I occasionally observe the permanently stoned workers, parents, and students around town. I psychically see a blue fog around the heads of people under the influence of pot. With 60 percent of the diet in this country consumed as chemical fake food and prepared meals, our neurology craves just one more fix to maintain our avoidant mindset. We are drugged. The terminally online addiction certainly crept into my life more slinkily and stillfully than I'd noticed. I claim the Neptunian mindset of an addict. My addiction is the addiction itself. Addiction to the transmitters is produced when I am addicted to a behavior and avoid a conscious mindset.

Two weeks ago, I intuited that I had become one of the terminally online populations. Ordering cool stuff on Etsy, Zappos, or Amazon dosed me with the comfort of endorphins I was healthfully creating through nature and silence. As an addict's addict, I am cross-addicted to not being addicted to my online circus. Now I'm practicing remembering how to sleep well sans the addiction to online stuff at night. I'll let you know how it goes; let us pray.

Some words are holographic to me. They are so rich and inclusive that I almost smell them. They enrich the topic from so many different angles of the senses. Addiction is one of those words. The disturbingly misguided practice of forcing a kundalini experience or using drugs or alcohol to achieve a desired level of experience out of the norm sometimes results in the experience but only of a physical nature. No true enlightenment comes from forcing the mind. Enlightenment is a virtue of the soul and evolves, as does one's point of evolution. Neither make light of nor ignore in ignorance the lessons of illness, even small irritations.

> *We seem to fall under a spell of our own making, ignorant of apparent facts or truths outside of the emotional time zone we have created.*

For these teachers are manifestations of where we are vulnerable to unconscious emotional desire and fatalistic beliefs. If the Diagnostic and Statistical Manual, the DSM, is a great ocean, we all dip our toe in it at times, and we float in it for an entire lifetime, perhaps. We are all a bit off, an expression of other than the norm to one degree or another. We all have an addiction, even if it's just being addicted and not having one. The decrees we espouse as truth will materialize in one life or another.

Addictions cloak these truths and seek emergence from the depths of misery. Addictions feel miserable because they attach our soul to the Earth plane, and the time-space limitations create restrictions. The thinking about needing more of it phase, leading up to the acting out of the addiction period, demonstrates this misery in feelings and all the physical discomfort. Addictions involve us feeding a lonely process of trying to fill up a bottomless pit with assumed security.

If we do not recognize our own addictions, we see them as mirrored in others' behaviors. Our level of denial reflects the discomfort we observe and feel. I noticed my own denial when I am at first observing myself running from an unpleasant feeling and pointing to the acting out in others. It never fails to amaze me how insidious this cycle is for myself. The mind is basic and animalistic. It searches for threats and disruptions so as to protect its status quo.

Most neural patterns set in childhood control the actions and belief systems of the adult. I like the recovery term adult child. This refers loosely to adults acting out with emotion during addictive cycles, but I use it to define all of us. As adults, the mind does not differentiate between it what encoded during formative years and what it is programmed this morning. We are all adult children in that sense. The mind will lie to us, the heart never will.

Only the intuitive heart tells the truth. Our gut instinct primarily alerts us to danger, but our intuitive heart-centered responses can prevent irrational reactions. Indeed, this is a learned behavior that Buddhism addresses through practices of meditative awareness and detachment from emotion. I find it unnerving how easily we protect our perceptions and project them onto others. We seem to fall under a spell of our own making, ignorant of apparent facts or truths outside of the emotional time zone we have created.

Have you noticed how quickly emotions change? My counselor says that if I feel bad, just wait twenty minutes. We don't always catch that moment of the shift, but we react to the feel better or the feel worse sensation as if it's just part of the atmosphere. How much control do we have over the process? Consciousness and awareness of the shift centering simplifies the complexity of the emotional mood. When I am adulting, I respond rather than react.

The elephant in the room pops out of the same closet housing the skeletons. All families hide their secrets. All families identify the elephant as someone else's issue. He is the projection personified. Hold my beer, watch this. My husband says that is the beginning of many ER visits. The elephant in the room of alcohol-addicted families is skilled at holding its breath, releasing the stale air only after an obvious crisis evokes that obviousness, the arcane secrets, the unavoidable exit of those skeletons.

Addiction is a family disease. We treat it by hoisting the addict onto the elephant and dancing with his addictions into the arms of blame. But where do we go from here? We can learn and cognate only that which connects us to emotional, spiritual, or mental cognitive issues. The body physically takes cues from the three other energy bodies because it is dense and Earthy. When our neurality, our brains and minds, have the neuro-receptors and etheric receptors to be capable of receiving higher intel, only then can we learn and evolve.

Something cannot connect to nothing. Similar to Buckminster Fuller's geodesics, one point connects to a second, and the third point connects all three triangularly. This demonstrates also how we evolve. What we know connects to what is already, what is newly presented, creating the energy for the encoding of the illuminated energies. In order to create and accomplish, one needs a structural foundation. We cannot haphazardly grow without something to connect to.

Consider the balancing evolution of reticence as the mind seeks confirmation of the new by connecting it to its foundation. Leaps in consciousness may indeed promulgate these opportunities of the mind to newness. I write often about how we become ourselves so slowly, in increments of discoveries and evolution of the soul's journey in form. This is a natural process which cannot be rushed. The temporal aspect of Earth life necessitates the physical experience of emotional uncoveries from our souls and our true selves.

Do we truly become someone different? It appears that we do, in the sense that growth from childhood to adulthood emphasizes recognition of our faults and successes who we aspire to be. It's rather simple, actually. The grace of growth allows this thoughtful evolution of recognizing who we are in a world of infinite possibilities.

In astrology, we address the archetype of Chiron to reveal what we have yet to heal. We are often given family and social situations which shine light on these issues, usually making them worse for the benefit of healing. Children may have parents who act out in childish ways, opening wounds and requiring healing. This feels so unfair, so treacherous and unfulfilling that we usually retreat to the safe emotional spaces learned in childhood. These portals to retreat open many doors all of which invite adulting at some point later in time.

Chiron was the wounded healer, the centaur, whose wound caused him not to be able to heal himself but could heal others. Children seek security, comfort, answers to unknown fears, and so much more that no parent can perfectly fill all of those spaces. The child within, the parent, the wounded person, seeks its own comfort. When arguing with another, perhaps we can relate more compassionately if we remember our own wounds. Arguments are actually between the unresolved childhood wounds of each person.

We tend to demand our own way, retreating to our childhood safe, happy place when those ways are not magnified and manifested. Our egos live in the emotional body and are never fully satisfied. The seven deadly sins and all of their family members force themselves upon the free will of others through the magnetism of pain and fear generated from childhood wounds. I am amazed at how selfish my own demands are during an argument. The only way to experience physical life is through our own selves, our perceptions, our beliefs, our interactions with the world.

We mute our voices and dim our lights when childhood wounds slam on the brakes during these experiences. Interactions with others demonstrate our wounds when we dismiss, forcibly act out, or negate our feelings. Others usually know more about our childhood wounds than we do. Our chronic inability to see them and our fear of what will happen once they are known to our conscious mind thwarts true healing. The subconscious knows all. It continually presents clues about our nature and perhaps stimulates our personalities curiosity to dig a bit deeper.

I am convinced that when folks argue, the arguing is the unfilled empty space, the unfilled needs, the fears and all of the unresolved issues from our childhood experiences. We are most vulnerable when we sleep, and when our conscious mind is discerning, discernment is mentally at rest. We are also most vulnerable when we are awake and unaware of our conscious options and self-protective behavior. As physical beings in the animal bodies housing our mind, spirit, and soul, our neuronal transmissions during stress, our limbic system reacts in a primal animal-like way.

We freeze, flight, and then fight if necessary. Arguments engage these same neutral mechanisms until our frontal brain's discernment calms the reactivity into response rather than reaction. We are only as good as our neurons. These powerful emotion-based reactions over stimulate the adrenal glands as they prepare us for a battle, real or not. The same limbic response to imagining battles acts as if we're encountering a bear in the woods. We act the comic, presenting impersonations of ourselves, roasting our human faults on the fires of others' opinions, but authentically removing us from the stage.

Addiction and family-of-origin recovery work is the deglamorization of emotional thought, form, and karmic obligations hidden from the conscious mind. The unconscious irritation of repeating discomforting and dysfunctional behavior profits the soul's desire to finish old business and illuminates its passage into the personality. Our Chiron placement points to what we can so clearly teach others but cannot recognize that we ourselves have disengaged in the learning process.

Chiron, the centaur wounded healer, could heal everybody but himself. Our Chironic wounds run deep and dark. The thorn is in our side, which will not come out because we cannot find it. Glamour is the sticky emotional glaze polluting clarity of mind. It is worldly and deceivingly attractive to the lower three chakras. Glamour subsides only with the mental stress of recognizing its falsehoods. Glamour is insidious, alluring and self-centered. It is the base draw of all addictions.

Addiction is always to protect the wounded inner child. I often remark that we cannot become anything else save our true soul-infused authentic selves. As we act out roles on this path, addiction demands we latch onto the most sensual role to feed its insatiable demands. Recovery involves conscious recognition of these damaging roles and detachment from their control. It's truly awful, frightening work.

Spirit and guidance offer us hints about our nature and the nature of life. We oft times wonder why we do not recall receiving answers to our ponderosities while those very answers are right in front of us. Our emotional glamours and intellectual illusions demand the attention better put towards a reticent discernment of those answers. Nature has no fear of her destructive power. She produces and allows to thrive before destroying all of her creations.

Physical life cycles through her patterns. We are born, live and die, as do all of her creations. The moon shines equally on all things. Its dependent and receptive nature manifests only from the sun's light. It is the closest bright orb and shining peace in the sky above us. Its essence is feminine and fertile. The moon impregnates the dark, the occult, with the arcane. It hides from us during the day's sunlight hours, pressing us to await its gradual entrance during the hours of our dreaming.

zoliartexoticamontana.com/music
"Never Too Old To Heal"

Your Questions Answered: Why are all addictions the same?

All addictions, to me, are the same. The reason they're the same is it's all about what's in our heads. Nobody's going to have an addiction if they haven't thought about it first. It's like if I'm sitting in front of the TV and I know there's an eclair in the refrigerator, and I love eclairs, and I didn't plan on eating it. The more I think about that, the more I'm going to want to eat it. Sooner or later, the emotions can take over and go to hell with it. I'm going to go eat it anyway. And when we do that, then here come all the emotions, "Why did I do that, I don't know. And oh, now I ate it. It lasted twenty seconds and now it's gone."

This is the nature of humanity. We come here to overcome ourselves. That's the only thing we come in to overcome. We have this physical body, then we have the astral emotional body, and right next to it, we have the etheric sheath. But it is the astral body that is so difficult to work with because we're still stuck in the Atlantean lesson of starting to feeling emotions.

We did it so well we have not quit. And that is the basis for all addiction. And addiction is the thought of doing it. If someone is addicted to a heavy drug or alcohol or with a real physical addiction, I think the neurology might take over there. The energies take over to where it's not a thought anymore. It's just all emotion.

Look what happens when you get in a crowd situation. And what's happening now all over the world? People are losing their shit. They will just walk up and shoot somebody. In a crowd situation, everybody's acting the same. These mirror neurons take over. But what happens is the emotions take over, and it is animal instinct. We live in these animal bodies. This makes me nuts because it's like, can't I get past it? Look how close we are to orangutans who have 99 percent of our DNA matching exactly.

People don't believe in evolution and say the Garden of Eden happened. I think both those things happened in some way. We are living in animal bodies. Though the Masters of Wisdom have evolved their body past the fourth-degree initiation of becoming a Master into the fifth and the sixth, they're not in animal bodies anymore with the emotions controlling them.

We're stuck. So, how do you get out of that? Meditation and service. To have a prayerful life inside of the self. To look for compassion. That Ho'oponopono prayer is so beautiful with that. All the world religions have ways of overcoming the emotions in whatever way you want to see that. But it's a sickness of humanity. We're crazy people, clearly. The last time I was in Italy, about twenty years ago, I saw a tombstone and had seen it before. It's in one of the famous cemeteries.

And it said, *I was as you are, you will be as I am.* And that is memento mori, my favorite thing that reminds me to live for the day. Remember that you are mortal, and take advantage of what is here. What the Masters say about this is, "Nobody can really see into the future because God plays dice, but it's also planned exactly from the beginning." That dichotomy is something that we don't understand, but it's true because everything is really in the present.

We get addicted to thinking about the past, trying to fix it, trying to be comforted by it. Then we want to plan the future. How much of that really happens? Not much. Then, we put the fears into the future. If we are really just present in the moment, that is what reality is. That's the real reality, and it spreads out laterally instead of moving forward and backwards.

Chapter 11:
Interconnection & Accepting Help

If I will not help myself or accept help from others, I probably deserve whatever drama I've created from my ego. Why do we expect more than the lesser gods of our race for accolades upon personal effort and accomplishment? Those lesser gods, namely the Masters of Wisdom, work tirelessly night and day to ameliorate the collective process and progress and balance from the damages we inflict upon others, the planet, and ourselves. While so many of the New Age philosophers claim power and independence from Source, declaring their single ability to manifest what they desire, perhaps they should depart from the spiritual agnosticism and seek reticent concern for the outcome of their demands.

It is that we humans are still so cloaked and internalized by our animal natures that we act like animals at times and not the good parts. Aspiring to change is not equal to pretending to have the aspired ability to enact without collaboration with the lesser gods of our plane. Indeed, by ourselves, we do nothing. As long as we do what we want, what we want will never happen in the long run. The wants are the desires.

Each one of us has something to say which could change the course of someone else's life. When we find our own voice, our true voice, it will be unique to us. This is rather miraculous to me as I see us all as one force, one group soul. How is it then that we are gifted with the voice of the soul, special and specific to who God created us to be and to become? That voice begins in the cave of the heart, the soul's Earthly home from which the authentic self evolves.

Is it true that we all have our prices? How much would it take for me to be bought out to save what I value? Oh wow, here we go. How many of us would say, well, I can't be bought? What if we had a sick child or a valued career? So, we do have a price, but what bothers us about that is the almighty dollar, the avarice and greed behind the callousness.

We are in a deep, dark, evil place. In truth though, we are here to spiritualize the matter comprising our physical world. To do that, to raise the energetic signature of matter, we have to shoot our free will into the material world because the material world is run by the feminine energies. Wait a minute, what did I just say? Am I accusing women of being evil? Not at all. The female polarity is the yin piece comprising the physical world.

That's why women were considered evil. Back when Lucifer was incarnating on this planet during the Atlantean time and went dark because of his identification with material things, he became them himself, and he became Satan. Lucifer was a high being from Saturn who originally sacrificed himself to drop to Earth. The agreement he made was to offer Earth the skills to manage and develop the material world. That is Saturn on a high level. He was a Master at the sciences, but he fell into addiction and power, creating pain and control over everything.

The main thing he did was take away power from women. And look at what's still happening. Women are not allowed even to be seen in some countries unless they're totally covered. Women are learning to present powerfully without demeaning men. The abused become the abuser when the love intuitive heart is not acted out. We are actually on track, but far from harmony between the sexes. I see a brilliant future!

Wherever you are, you have to go by the rules of that society. So, the world that rules us still is the world that Satan, satanic energy, set up. That's why women are considered evil because feminine energy, the negative polarity, is being decimated by pollution and greed. Did you know that the feminine energies rule material things? Think about that.

But all is not lost, maybe misunderstood. In Orthodox Judaism, women sit separately from men. That is not such a bad thing when you think about it because when you are opening your energies in prayer, what else are you opening up to receive? My Hunka family of the Lakota Sioux practices strict protocols around females and the moon times. My niece reports that she has seen men pass out during our Sundance if a female is there who is on her moon. Females bleed monthly with no blood loss; it's weird but hugely powerful and misunderstood. Isn't it interesting, the things that have been lost and perverted? Is it really against women to say they can't sit with men or have to participate in the sacred bath, the Mikvah?

I thought this was all just oppressive B.S. until I was adopted by my family on the Rosebud Sioux Reservation. I learned and humbled myself when having to put it in a sacred perspective. My niece just related that she will be on her moon during our 2023 Sundance. My great-niece could not cut the tree because she began having her moon a couple of months ago. A young girl, one not yet a woman, is required to cut the tree used for the Sundance.

These are the things that have been lost. I find it fascinating because people now perceive some notions about women during their moon time as abusive. You know, they had to be separate on their moon time, but they don't realize it was because women were powerful. I find it fascinating that the negative is prominent, but we don't know the other side. We don't know the other side because the past 2,500 years have been under the Yang energies, where males were disallowed from feeling emotions.

And when women say they can't stand being around men, I ask them what kind of man they were during their male lives? Were they one of those?

But back to the price thingy. I guarantee you I have a price like everybody else. Why I got out of the music business, why I got out of doing art shows, the almighty dollar just squashed my creativity. The Italians have a phrase, *paese que vai, usanza que trova*. When in Rome, do as the Romans do. As we adapt to our society's norms and values, we will have to pay Caesar his due. My price is learning how much I owe him and how much it costs to get my work out there.

zoliartexoticamontana.com/music
"In My Last Life I Was a Cow"

Your Questions Answered: How do I know who to connect with?

There are eight billion people on this planet. Try to choose who's going to be in your life. That's a little better choice. And at times, it just seems cruel that I'm saying to myself I can't have that person in my life because it threatens my emotional sobriety.

The fact is, I could probably drink a glass of wine I'm not going to want anymore. I'm not an alcoholic, but I'm an addict brain, or I'm just so aware of what addiction is. At some point, the substance has to be curtailed. I used to be a compulsive eater. I wasn't obese. I was just dumb, and I was eating too much. Then I'd go exercise like crazy. But the only way that I stopped it, and I never figured out where I got this from, maybe Buddhism. I was at the farm one day. I said, "You know what? I'm going to quit trying to control my diet. I'm just going to watch what I eat. How do I feel when I eat it?" And I fixed it.

It just melted away. I became aware of my behavior, and that's the answer to all addiction. The mayor of New York, Eric Adams, announced they were going to start teaching meditation in school, thank God. They're doing that in prisons, and it is changing people's lives. I don't agree with everything he says, but that is brilliant. You can't argue with that.

So, once again our awareness is key. Wake up. Just be aware of who you are. When I do that, my life goes great. I honestly don't know how my Master deals with me. I mean, he puts up with so much stuff. The other day when I said, "You know, I don't think I'm doing so great with this."

He replied, "You're doing fine with it. Just zip it. Shut up." Really, that's how they talk. They don't put up with any crap. They're not trying to make you feel bad.

How do you know the difference between co-dependency and partnership?

Codependency is different from interdependency. When you're in a partnership with somebody, and you are interdependent with them, you are depending on trusting them. With codependency, there is no trust. Codependency says, "I know everything about your life, and I can tell you what you need to do. I can take care of you. I can do this and that." You are other-focused.

With interdependence, you are independent, but you are working together with somebody else. On the other hand, codependency doesn't have any boundaries. It has no limits. It runs all over choice. It's just absolute panic.

I say I'm a recovering codependent. When I was younger, as an autistic artist, I really didn't know who I was. But that's what the life journey is about. I was a kid. I didn't know, and so I was focused on taking care of other people, which made me valuable. And being codependent says that that my self-worth is dependent on you.

My counselor says, "You will not get along 70 percent of the time. But you have to learn to do it lovingly and in an interdependent way where you are reticent and you don't react. That reactivity is the codependent panic. And codependency is a basis of all addiction."

We all have codependent relationships in our lives at some point, and maybe it's because we're threatened. I don't know, but I think becoming aware of our behavior and learning more about who we are as human beings, that sort of authenticity just flattens codependency. Those two things cannot live in the same room because when you're authentic, you're not relying on anyone else's opinion or requirements of you.

Codependency can be totally irrational. It makes no sense. Other people can see it. But to the person that's doing the codependent behavior, it feels life-threatening not to do it.

A nurse friend of mine says nurses are the most codependent people there are. And I think I agree with her in just in one sense; because you are dependent upon the nurse, and the nurse is the ultimate caretaker. And I do know a couple of nurses that are blatantly codependent, and they are amazing nurses. Who cares? I mean, that's their thing. That's what they do. But when you bring your vocation into your home life, or in a relationship outside of your vocation or profession, that is a boundary violation.

I know with myself that blatant codependency comes up in me when I'm insecure. And I say, I'm not a really secure person, but that's part of my charm. I'm always doubting myself. I'm always wondering and always wanting to do better. I think a lot of people can relate to that.

I think it is an artsy-fartsy kind of thing. Are there codependent scientists? Sure. It has to do with how we're raised. Who depends on you? Who do you depend on? I wrote this song years ago called "Codependent Again." I'm alive, but I just don't know how. I went far from home, but oh, if I'd known, they're still living inside of me now. So, you have to face yourself; wherever you go, there you are.

Most of the really co-dependent people I've met are not comfortable with themselves at all. They are the kind of people that can't be alone. That's a crazy kind of dynamic there: codependency and aloneness. I think codependency can escape from trying to interact with other people by being alone, but it's always other-focused. If it's alone, it's not going to be comfortable.

I'd say codependency is a lack of care for yourself and over-care for other people. They probably don't need it.

A lot of parents get that way with their children. Parenting is interdependent. And it can be codependent. Anything can be. It requires balanced care for yourself and others and not just going too far either way.

There's that balance again. We never really get it, though we try. An example is overwork, over-care, over this, over that. We're swinging all the way to one side, overdoing everything. And we're either going to get sick, exhausted, or pissed off. Something's going to set us off, and we're going to drink, we're going drug, we're going do something to get us to swing all the way to the other side. And, of course, the beauty of life is to be in those moments when we do feel balanced, when we are at peace with our self.

My own struggles with codependency just came from not knowing who I was, and it drove me crazy. When I was in my twenties, I would always say, "I want to develop a core personality that I can take around with me." And I've got that now, but that took me a hell of a long time. I was a flaming codependent. My whole life depended on other people's opinions of me, what I looked like, what my work was, where I lived, and how I was in other people's eyes.

When I bought the farm in Olympia, that changed my whole life. Leaving Alabama was a really good step for me. I didn't do well in Alabama. It didn't accept much change, and we did not get along. But it was a karmic situation I was in. So, for me to get out of Alabama, to get out of the southeast United States, as much as I do love it there, it was a very healthy move for me.

I moved to the West Coast from the East Coast. Then, I started developing confidence with a farm, raising my cattle, and meeting people that I cared for. But it took a long time. I'd say I was probably in my fifties before I really started to get it. I had some great counselors. I did a lot of counseling. Oh my gosh. I had a lot of good groups. I got a lot of help, and I say that I went through a twenty-year recovery process for codependency.

Codependency is my main addiction. I drank a little bit. I did some alcohol. I smoked some weed. I did some coke. I didn't do that much. It wasn't my main thing. I would binge drink, but my main addiction was not knowing who I was or how I fit into the world.

I think that's the underlying issue for many, many people. That's why I hope that when I put out personal things, people will think, "Wow! I thought I was messed up, but, boy, she was pretty messed up too." And I hope it makes them feel better.

Not only that, but it's a learning process because we're not taught that these things are changeable. We think we if we don't fit a certain mold, we're broken.

What really helped me were the CODA (Codependents Anonymous) meetings. I went to hundreds of those meetings. They changed my life. When I first sat at a meeting, this was back in the eighties when addiction recovery became very, very big, and there were meetings all over the place, all the time, with hundreds of people. It was amazing in Olympia, and I went to a doubleheader one night. I went to one at four and another one at six.

There probably were fifty people at each meeting. And every time I went, I would hear maybe one thing that clicked. Sometimes, I would go, and I wouldn't say a darn thing. I would just listen and go, "How did they know my story?" Because we're so similar. I wrote a song about that, the "Children of Recovery." That whole recovery album, *Never Too Old to Heal*, is about the healing that can happen in those meetings. They're amazing.

Chapter 12:
Intention and Repetition

I hope that I write so simply that each of you resonate with my words, saying to yourself, "I already knew that!" We can only be taught what we remember from our soul. There really is nothing new under the sun. These pages can only remind us what has been forgotten. The soul is a Master on its own plane. The subconscious mind knows all we have done, who we are, our efforts and our prayers. We are indeed divine in that sense but should give all honor to the soul within, which is God's presence.

The intention behind each action is what creates Skanda, the Buddhist word for karma. This is the resulting effect of our thoughts and our actions. All similar actions are not necessarily rooted in the same intention. We absolutely harvest the actions we commit upon the physical plane of being. Errant thoughts seek form as a negative behavior, as intention to do harm manifests in discordance. The genesis of intention's cause is long gone by the time we encounter the actual effect of what we thought, what we did in our mind, and what happened, then pointing the quiet finger at someone else.

When I do this, I am reminded to back it up to when and where my original thought was created, the errant behavior and the resulting event. Maitreya says, "Most people are dead or dying." That's a rich statement. We are so out of touch with our soul. Some folks appear not to have access to the brilliance of the soul, acting only from the physical and emotional bodies. We certainly have a lot to learn, but that's why we're here, right? Old habits die hard because they are just that, habits habitually practiced.

Perhaps we require a fun ritual for the old habits that died a hard-earned death, for those habits were the finger-whacking stern nunnies teaching through pain and shame. I suggest a New Orleans Jazz band funeral offering a nice horn section, parasols and an ebony casket for the dead habit. After we reach New Orleans Cemetery and funeralize the dead, we can let loose with a bawdy, loud second line celebration on our way to the new life. Laissez les bon temps...

> *These are places, beings, and issues we just need to leave alone. Walk away. God's world contains all things. Please attend to your spider senses, your situational awareness, your intuition and common sense.*

I can have clearly defined personal boundaries and still practice non-judgmental behavior. Perhaps we could get along better as a nation if we recognize that the left or the right are attached to the same bird. Both wings are needed. We cannot fly with only one wing. When we refer to ourselves as I and you as you, should the I not be in small caps and the U not be in big caps? Some things are actually so dark that no amount of light can penetrate their edges.

These are places, beings, and issues we just need to leave alone. Walk away. God's world contains all things. Please attend to your spider senses, your situational awareness, your intuition and common sense. Not all battles need to be fought. Wisdom and courage also involve knowing when to avoid the war to fight another day.

Easter actually celebrates and commemorates Jesus's fourth-degree initiation. Maitreya brought into life the dead corpse of Jesus for his sixth-degree initiation. On Ascension Sunday, 50 days later, Easter denotes Maitreya's seventh-degree initiation, the Advocate of the Holy Spirit's descent into the availability to us after this. Before Jesus left, others had to stand in to draw down the Holy Spirit. We now have access to it, 24-7.

We use what we have to get what we want. We cannot give what we do not have. My precious Mom and I danced to different music, each arguing with our karma and demanding that the other change the tune. We adored each other but saw the world very differently. We all endure relationships that are both confusing and conflictual. Our personality and astral ray structures grate on the soul's desire to relieve our suffering by demanding we get our own way.

My own example may serve to enlighten. Mom could not give me what she herself did not have to give. I never received the security or vulnerability of our community. I just didn't fit in. She tried so hard. What a great gal! When I presented my vulnerability to Mom's acerbic scorpionic personality and Aries moon, she weaponized my vulnerability. I translated that as sabotage, but now know that was her effort to teach me to be strong. Painful results are rarely born of good intent.

She simply knew no other way. She saw me more as a sister to compete with at times than a daughter to nurture. But that was from a past life, see? This was raw survivalism for her. God gave me a mom whose personality flipped on a dime from loving to treacherous. She just didn't know any other way. I say mom didn't get the help she deserved; she got Valium. This was the madman era. My parents were born in 1921. They were part of the greatest generation. God wanted me to learn what I had not previously learned in other lives.

Co-Dependency And Montana Mini-Meditation

This morning, I found myself engaged in an old practice of pointing my finger at someone else's behavior. This behavior was incredibly codependent in my mind. How did I deserve this treatment? What came to me was the thought that the mother of all addictions is codependency. We become fuse-bonded with the idea that we and others are unsafe to know. We then become mini managers of other people's behaviors to protect ourselves from our own behaviors. We become responsible for their responsibilities, ignoring ours.

We project our insecurities onto others, imagining they cannot live without our care or our opinion. Codependency is the disease of human nature as prevalent as breathing. I apparently breathe it in a lot. Are there levels of codependency? Of course. Fear, uncertainty and unresolved childhood trauma are triggers. Habitual behaviors of controlling others, micromanaging, criticizing, enabling and overstepping boundaries create the stage for codependent acting out.

All addictions begin with codependency, which presents when we know more about other people than we know about ourselves. We can list their faults and behaviors while unable to identify them in ourselves. How delicious is that? How do we break the cycle of unconscious behavior, which serves no good and holds us in the behavior prison of our own making? How do we cycle from stress to occasional flashes of awareness, then back again to the stress?

Seva is a selfless service we offer without exacting due service. It gives freely with no expectation of recognition or reward. The left hand does not know what the right is doing.

The Sikh religion bases its spiritual practice on the foundation of service, of seva. All spiritual paths allow us to find our own rhythm of giving. The ego argues with desire to be the first, the best, and have the most. I'm uncomfortable when I catch myself in this stuff because I know the consequences, but do it anyway.

I feel better and more peaceful when focussing on the good of the whole instead of my own problems. When I can groove to the music from my soul, I feel no desire to change the music to a discordantly distracting tune.

That's a boundary. Where do I stop, and where do you start? The personality doesn't know; it just keeps pushing. The soul will demonstrate that line in the sand, protecting the mind, body, spirit— the dumb personality—from the negativity of martyrdom. I know you already got this, but humor me because codependency and boundaries are my life work, my life lessons. You know the feeling that happens all too often. Here comes an opportunity to do good for a higher purpose, but I'll need to modify my self-centeredness to make the work real.

I'll have to rein in my desire body, suck it up, control my impulse to get a little irritated over what I have to give in time or stuff and do what I know is right. It really challenges me sometimes because I want to do what I want to do. Fair enough. How do I resolve these feelings? I've spent decades trying at least to train the codependent nature with the recognition of when my own boundaries are violated.

It's just crazy how often we say, do, or push our own will onto others' landscapes, but I digress. It's embarrassing to admit how self-centered I can be when I actually know better. Seva is 50 percent of the solution. The other half is meditation and prayer. Okay, I know you don't want to join a cult and sit cross-legged until your bowels explode. I can't do that either. So, what kind of meditation can we as westerners do? Here in Montana, we still have cowboys, range riders, and gals who shoot elk with crossbows.

I actually do own twenty pairs of cowboy boots and hats telling lies to each other in my closet. No, wait a minute, I really do wear the boots. I'm not them. I'm not one of these people who have been raised in this wonderful environment. I'm now a Yankee, a transported Southerner, but I'm also a Montanan, okay? Raising a small fold of Scottish Highland cattle in Olympia for several decades did not qualify me to write cowboy poetry and get my boots out of the corral.

But that's the deal. A Montana meditation is waking up in the morning in the crisp, beautiful air, sitting on my deck with a cup of joe and pondering gratitude. Just feeling, smelling the air, listening to the birds. During the day, I manage my meditations by setting aside my iPad and iPhone. I practice noticing my monkey mind demanding I pay attention to those have to do's rolling across my mental landscape like a dust storm pestering the gulch.

Oh yeah, in Montana, we have gulches. In Appalachia, we had hollers. Maybe you call them valleys or something else. When my mini-Montana meditations go well, I feel refreshed. My egoic mind thinks it's got the attention it demanded because I noticed it.

zoliartexoticamontana.com/music
"To The Trees"

Your Questions Answered: Why do I have resistance to service?

Service isn't that hard, really. You do it all the time in your family. Maybe you work a bit at a service organization or have created your own way to get out of your own way.

However, it can be really hard to do when your own way appears to color the way of service as being something you might not want to do at that minute. But it's supposed to sting a bit, right? That stinging is the ego's rant. Just ignore it. Seva is sacrificing that ego to the higher good or the common good.

Is it martyrdom? Is it self-pity? You may indeed feel like that, but don't let it fool you. I think that self-pity is actually the lowest form of self-care. That's kind of surprising, isn't it? But I've observed it in myself and others. When we feel sorry for ourselves, we're really trying to take care of that little child inside of us that didn't get what it needed or wanted. That can be insatiable. No parent can give you everything, and we shouldn't have to ask for everything, but as kids, we're insatiable.

And that self-pity and the resistance to service, that's the little kid stamping its foot. Maybe it's not so bad if it's left on the back porch like the recycling. That little sting of self-pity is us noticing us. It's the good and kind part, tapping the ego on the head and saying, "Pay attention, we're going to adult now." (That's a verb, by the way.) I think as long as we don't indulge in its attention-seeking drama, acting out a little self-pity can lead us to the path of service.

Codependency is so ingrained in us that we take it for granted, but it is really a tool to learn how to connect with our soul through the pain of feeling how only connecting to our ego hurts. We're so darn pleasure pain centered that our emotions ruin us; our emotions run us. When we're constantly demanding that our ego be fed, that is insatiable. But remember, service is divine love. It has no beginning or end. It flows freely and beautifully. *Here we go again,* you're thinking. Is she going to point at that iceberg again? That iceberg of codependency which uses our pointing finger to blame others when we have four fingers pointing back at ourselves? If I can only catch myself when I indulge in the balance gone game, I find the codependent iceberg melting a tiny bit, or maybe a little more.

With so much of our own behaviors underwater, unnoticed to the emotion that is, how is it that we can even begin to develop an awareness of what is hidden below? Well, welcome to Earth. That's just what we do. We kind of have to settle into that. We explore our behavior. We watch ourselves watching ourselves. We try. That's the big thing. Try. I jokingly say the people who think we're going to heaven or anywhere else when we get there, does God say, "How much did you weigh? What did you eat?" No, I think that God might ask, "Did you try? Did you put out effort?" Today, I plan on trying not to blame what gets in my way.

I plan on trying to own my own crap a little better. We'll see how it goes.

Why does karma seem random?

It seems random because we don't notice the good stuff. We only notice we get all jacked up about the bad stuff. Like, why did I meet this person I was so drawn to, and then we had these awful things happen? Well, we're emotional creatures, usually, and karma is a very emotional situation because it involves some other time and place, and we're not there anymore.

And when these feelings come back, a lot of times, the feelings of that lifetime filter in with it.

There are a lot of pieces that come together that wouldn't come together if we hadn't had that specific karmic coexperience. But it seems random because certain things seem to just come out of the blue. Everything is karmic because we are whatever we think, whatever we say, even our dreams; those create equal and opposite reactions. Though not every relationship is karmic. We create new karma all the time. That's why we're asked to be harmless as much as possible.

And that's where the trying comes in; just to keep trying to do better.

That's the main thing. It gets back to that thing that I harp on about the seven deadly sins in the backpack that we get when we are born that we carry our whole life. We never really get it. Unless we're about to become a master, high initiate, there are very few on the planet, but we just have to try. We have to keep moving forward, and sometimes, as inching forward, we make big leaps. But it's all related to service and what we do here in this life to serve humanity, to serve something.

And it all gets back to our sole purpose. What did we come here to do? People get stuck on the bad stuff. They're looking there on purpose.

We all feel undeserving. Something shitty happened, and it's just like, I didn't deserve that. Well, maybe you did, maybe you didn't, but what are you going to do with it?

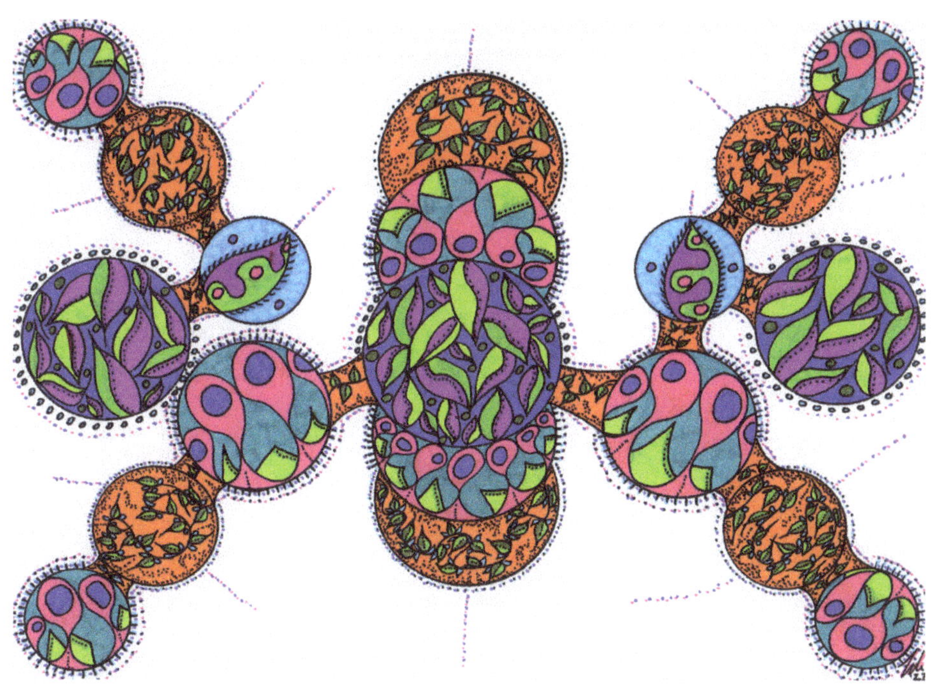

Chapter 13:
Reality is a Spectrum

There are four levels we cannot measure. Coming into consciousness, and all this stuff pulls together to the truth. Hope keeps us going. God knows what we are going to do even though we have free will. Follow free will and intuition, and know you are not crazy.

I address my autism in my book, *The Reality Pirate's Journal*, so I feel no need to dive too deeply into those waters now. However, I am passionate about encouraging others on the wide spectrum to not only enjoy soaking in those waters but perhaps gear up to explore the depths. I was diagnosed at age 63. Before then, I knew something might be a little cray-cray, but I wasn't sure what it was. I was hyper-creative, but certain things I just could not track.

But everything fell into place when I finally had comforting answers to my lifelong questions of why I was incapable of accessing areas that others found so easy. Looking back on my manner of communication, I find gaping holes in the signals sent and what I could receive. I still struggle with this, but I have learned to make eye contact and pause my reactions. Female autistics are usually diagnosed, if at all, later in life than the guys.

We communicate earlier and appear to have a more developed Broca's area in our brain than do the boys. At least, that's my theory. I feel joy in the comfort of researchers and therapists assuring autistics that the brain indeed can learn and can compensate for the lack of ability to understand facial signals. Autistics are manifest collectors and organizers of our own areas of interest. I giggle to notice my plethora of crystals, rocks, weird earrings, memento mori skulls, and way too many collections to name.

> *We laser focus on our area of interest while ignoring all else. This peculiarity has gifted me with the skills to produce huge volumes of work in my three areas of music, art, and writing. It's a true joy.*

We laser-focus on our area of interest while ignoring all else. This peculiarity has gifted me with the skills to produce huge volumes of work in my three areas of music, art, and writing. It's a true joy. I have been asked how I did all of this and how I continue to produce so much material. It's autism. That's a gift. Trust. ADD. That's my trifecta of accomplishment. I am smart, but not too smart to block out my love of the common man. I see myself as a simple me, and I hope you can see that in my work.

zoliartexoticamontana.com/music
"Kay Ee Mah"

Your Questions Answered: Can anyone learn to be a reality pirate?

It's kind of a fun club anyone can join. What you have to do is act it out in your own mind. I think we all do it at times. Like how somebody says, "Hey, where'd you just go? I was talking to you. Oh, you're off in a density somewhere." But as I wrote about the definition of reality pirating, compassion really is the foothold in it. We can't just do what we want and then wonder why things happen.

To me, the reality pirate concept is to explore other realities and other people's ways of being. Because if you get ten people in the room, they're all going to have different realities in some ways, but we have a shared reality. The psychopaths really can't share in that reality because it takes compassion, it takes temperance, it takes tolerance. I think Reality Pirate is saying that the five physical senses are not all that there is.

Reality is not what it used to be; it changes all the time. I'm a bit of a different person right now than I was when you and I started writing this. So, are you? Because everything changes all the time. It truly is the only constant, but we depend on the stability of the physical world to be able to maneuver through that. In other words, I can sit here and do a visualization and do a reality pirate, dream visualization or shamanic journey, and I can sit here, and the room will look the same when I come out of it.

That chair is still going to be there, and we count on that. When those things start morphing, if we could see the spaces between the molecules and the atoms, that's what the matrix is about. Now, you can go there. That's what LSD does. You can go there, and you can change your perception of how that works, but everything has a price. There are consequences for that. That's not my path. There are some people that choose drugs as a venue into other realities. You can take a quick Ayahuasca trip and then have the answers. But if you gain experience from doing that, you're going to have to come back and do it naturally. Sorry. It doesn't last.

And I know that's absolutely true. I joined the AMORC Rosicrucian Order in 1976. We are taught no shortcuts and that psychic and spiritual development open slowly because we must acclimate to those new ways. The physical body is dense and needs to be trained to accept higher energies.

That's not to say there are no benefits to such treatments. They're using it for trauma. And I think drugs have a wonderful application if used properly for trauma and for setting things right emotionally. But to try to use drugs and alcohol as a way to spiritually evolve and gain psychic power doesn't last. You have to come back and do it naturally.

It's a personal choice. You can't be here unless you're here. And I think being present in the body is a great gift. The more present I am, the more reality-based I am and that reality is the shared one that we have, plus the fifty years of work I've done dealing with other densities. That kind of fuses into a big ball of wax there, and I can make a candle out of that and burn that and give that to the world even when I'm not here. I just I don't think we can become anything other than what we are.

We have to wear a lot of hats. We have to try. We can make our hair blue, we can make our makeup this, we can wear funny hats. We can try on all these different density expressions, and that's fine. But sooner or later, we're going to have to come home to who we are. And I think when we see people that have done that, those are the real teachers. They're just quiet inside. And that's a Master to me. I aspire to that. If I ever get that, I'm sure everybody will know, but I'm not there.

Chapter 14:
Spiritual Work and Astrology:
A Map to Ourselves

When first pondering the language and numerical actions of one's astrological profile, it can feel like wandering around a foreign airport. The confusion stems from the combining of personal beliefs and habits with the soul's creation of aspects affecting the life one calls his own. I find it helpful to choose only a few of the natal chart's aspects to illuminate the path created by the soul before birth. For starters, the sun, moon, and position of the ascendant set the general tone of the chart.

Then, the nodes of the moon, the Chiron point, and the point of fortune fill in the spaces in between the first three big placements. The sun is the personality where we shine and present the active self to the outer world. If one is truly oneself, he will act out through his sun sign.

The moon is the emotional connection one has to one's inner self. It will demonstrate aspects from other lives and demand satiation of its feeling nature. It is more personal and private than the sun.

The ascendant defines what planet was rising, also called your rising sign, at the moment we took our first breath into this life. Oft times, others will see us as our rising sign rather than our Sun sign because the ascendant seeks to rise and to be seen. To grasp the connection among those three planetary indicators can be confusing at first, but the new language evolves in understanding as the feelings begin to connect. Just sit within it a while and perhaps start to notice how during the normal day These three aspects and planets talk to each other and to you.

I like to compare the twelve houses of the astrology chart to a school where transiting planets come in and out of the homeroom to reach and teach their lessons. Your homeroom is your natal chart; it is fixed. Those planets do not change. Some planets spend years in the homeroom sharing their lessons with other visiting planets, and the natal planets. The moon, for example, changes signs every couple days, demonstrating the flighty nature of emotion and its effect upon our feeling nature.

> *I like to compare the twelve houses of the astrology chart to a school where transiting planets come in and out of the homeroom to reach and teach their lessons. Your homeroom is your natal chart; it is fixed.*

Huge planets like Saturn spend many years in the room at times. It can feel like Saturn is at the lectern or even sitting in the back of the room, adjusting the behavior of other visiting planets as we experience their effects. Pluto, a small planet, actually defines a period similar to the other outer planets by spending eleven to thirty years in a sign. As with several other planets, Jupiter and Neptune, this so-called generation of people possess the Plutonian qualities or detriments defined by the sign Pluto is in at the time of their birth.

Neptune spends about fourteen years in a sign, and Jupiter spends about twelve. These populations can be seen when people behave in a collective way defining and expressing those particular qualities and detrimental society-changing behaviors. In the natal chart, Chiron defines where we are wounded to heal ourselves. Yet, we are so clear into insight of helping others and seeing others. The sign Chiron is in demonstrates where one helps, and the opposite sign reveals the wound. One has little or no insight into that denial until circumstances present the wounds as crises or continuing emotional conflicts.

The nodes of the moon, the moon's north and south nodes, show what we have come to learn and teach. The north node and its house will be Chironic in the sense that it feels unfamiliar, and so discomforting that we choose to run back to the south node and its house for comfort. The north node shows what we have not only avoided facing but also where we will find success once we dig deeply into its uncharted territory. The south node and its house show our past life accomplished focus and what we are so familiar with that others see us as its master.

It is what we do naturally. The planet Pluto is the errant, disruptive bad actor. Its sudden and dramatic explosions define change as revolutions leading to either evolution or rebellious negativity. Saturn is order, discipline, adulting, military, law enforcement and responsibility. When they oppose each other or even engage in conversation, sparks will fly. Pluto is the demanding, angry teen while Saturn is the demanding, responsible concerned adult.

Jupiter, just think of joy and abundance in the room. It will stimulate success through both literary and explorative pursuits. One can perhaps gain some extra pounds during a Jupiter period or see gains in projects. Neptune is the new age hippie of the zodiac. It rules dreamy creativity, psychic creations, and boundless exploration of other worlds. Neptune rules Pisces, who struggles with boundaries, distractions and addictive behavior of all sorts.

We are pressed to attend to what is in front of us on a daily basis, which is our Sun, Moon and Ascendant. Yet project onto the world our expression of the transiting planetary aspects. Who and what we are can be very different things. In astrology, we act upon our natal chart by what planets are in the homeroom. The who of us may be challenged with the boundary of maintaining its core values while challenged from externally shifting forces.

We are born in physical bodies to live a physical life while spiritualizing matter. Consciousness does not, as believed, create reality because consciousness IS reality. Awareness of our chart shines light on how to bring consciousness into these rather abstract forms. We have to try. Yes, try. A life spent in Neptunian addiction of drugs, alcohol, bizarre sexuality and behavior leads us nowhere.

Avoiding consciousness is a wasted life.

Let me run something by you. This goes against the religious teachings ingrained in our Christianity, as well as in several other religious doctrines. This is kind of weird, but thank you for humoring me. Just stay with me on this. All I ask is that you tune into your heart and just consider this as I present a possibility. Always check with your heart. I don't doubt that these beliefs are precious to the masses and cause much drama, war, separation of families and hatred.

But just try to consider the feelings that you will encounter that might be transformative rather than false. So here we go. Who is Satan? The name comes from the planet Saturn. Eighteen and a half million years ago, a Venusian being, that's somebody from Venus named Sanat Kumara, came to Earth called here by the Earth herself to create the races, rituals, and evolution of our species. Eighteen million years ago a great being of intelligence and light entered our world, and his name was Lucifer.

He entered into the reincarnational cycle of Earth and was destined to evolve our intellect. He sacrificed, I mean from Saturn; he sacrificed to be here as we all do from the great unknown. But his incarnation devolved him through the centuries to create a worship of himself, luring in millions of followers during the time of Atlantis. Lucifer was one of the eight great beings of our solar system.

He was the representative of Saturn, and he was perfectly skilled in educating and evolving humanity in the ways of the material world. He was a Master at these things. But as the other seven gods did not attach themselves so heavily to the material plane, Lucifer literally became the material plane. The Dark Lord's true purpose, which is evil, is to actually and truly hold in place the atomic and energetic structure of Earth, of the material world. During the final thousand years of Atlantis, Lucifer lost total control of his senses and taught that females were lower than low that they needed to be controlled and debased. This is evident even today when the female nature is depressed. The gods of technology and intellect rule, suppressing the female nature in men also, which is feeling.

Psychism considering the female virtues is not allowed. Saturn's astrological interpretation of energies includes rulership over the sign of Capricorn. Saturn is the planet of ambition and tangible results, persistent, permanent structures and conservative beliefs, timing delays, law enforcement, the military, fear and pain, discipline, barriers and self-control, as well as control over people and events. It holds things in place. These attributes are Capricornian and Aquarian, as it rules both sides.

That's surprising, isn't it? When these signs go negative, fascism and death are promulgated in society. Lucifer literally embodied this. In Atlantean times predating the sinking of that continent, the masses were like the Borg on the Star Trek series. They could not think for themselves. Lucifer bound a very large group of more evolved Atlanteans to his service, controlling all others. Mind you, the beings of light and the record-keepers on Atlantis had already begun transferring sacred tenets to Egypt for when the civilization would reinvent itself in that land. Just consider the pyramids.

But I'll tell you this. In December of 1944, Lucifer was packed off and sent back to Saturn. So, he is not here, but all his little minions are. Welcome to Earth.

Your Questions Answered: How do children learn spirituality?

In my understanding, what Benjamin Creme says in *Maitreya's Mission* and *Share International* magazine is that children should be allowed to develop naturally without glamours of dogma clouding their curiosity. They should ideally be allowed to ask questions when they are interested and capable of understanding at different ages. Don't program them with anything.

Creme called his son, boy, for the longest time. But I mean, he's kind of far above it all, as a fourth-degree initiate, way above us. But before age nine, kids really are just out there.

Then age nine to fourteen is a different focus. At age fourteen they have more of an adult brain, if I'm saying that correctly. But these children you see around you now will grow up in a world where if someone has liver disease, they will go into a clinic to have a liver grown out of their own cells. These kids will grow up in a world that has minimal, if any, war. Diseases will be fixed. Children will be taught more like the Montessori methods. They'll be taught as individuals based on their Rays and points of evolution. Imagine such a world! It is coming. Much will be taken into consideration for each child's education and health of mind, body and spirit. A new world is coming. Heed the light!

I think I was blessed when I was adopted into this family in Birmingham at the age of four months. Growing up Jewish, I never heard that there was a devil or that God hated me or that I was a sinner. When I went to grade school and heard about the devil, I thought it was the Tasmanian devil at Disneyland.

I didn't know. But I was blessed to have my nannies who raised me, these African American women, the goddesses I call them, who taught me quietly about Jesus, about Christ, and I learned from them. I've never published this, but it is very interesting. We grew up in the suburbs, my brother Bill and I, outside of Birmingham, in an area called Mountain Brook, "over the mountain," it is called. Bill and I grew up on ten acres; it was very quiet. Our parents were loving, wonderful people. Mom didn't have much education, but she really improved herself. She did crossword puzzles, she read stories, she took classes. And dad was just, in Catholicism, we call him a saint. Our vibrant home was filled with all kinds of people. Birmingham had a very diverse ethnic population due to the medical and educational folks coming into the University of Alabama in Birmingham. We had the florist and his boyfriend and their families, Jews, Christians, all kinds of people.

There was a large Greek community in Birmingham. I grew up knowing a lot of Greeks, Russians, the whole ball of wax. And there was a couple that came to the house a couple times when I was about, I'd say maybe, eight or nine because I remember I had feet pajamas on. (Remember those things? Those were great. We shouldn't have given those up.) But this man and his wife were sitting with Mama and Daddy in what I call the forbidden room, which was the living room. And we couldn't really go in there because it was the special room. The house was big enough anyway. But on this particular night, it wasn't quite dark, but I was getting ready to go to bed apparently, and I can still see myself padding in there to kiss my parents goodnight. Daddy said for some reason to "Tell Mr. And Mrs. So and So about the dreams you have, you know, the ones with the man?"

Now, my father never would have broached that subject. What pressed him to say that? The tall, elegant man had a presence about him. Perhaps he was a minister of sorts? He looked at me and asked me to tell him about my dreams. I said, "I've dreamed of a farmer. He was nice, and he had a little sheep."

"Really?" He pressed. "The farmer had sheep?" The adults were all sharing what-a-cute-kid look until I said.

"And the farmer was dressed in a long white dress holding like this stick. And he picked up one of the sheep. And he smiled at me. "

The elegant man almost dropped his drink. Leaning forward on the couch, he asked me if the man told me who he was. "He said his name was Yeshu, Yeshua something, and Joseph was his dad."

And all of a sudden, I had that full body feeling that I was in the presence of something. So, it scares the holy shit out of me to imagine how different my life would have been if the lord had not granted me this gift at an early age, I would have grown up without Christ. And I've had several experiences like this. I don't know why. It makes me feel almost sick, the humility of it.

Our neighbors across the road were the Harshes, wonderful people. Dr. Harsh and his wife were very strong Southern Baptists. They came over one day after my mom's daddy had passed and granny was sitting there, just this tiny little grieving woman. I will never forget Mrs. Harsh kneeling next to granny's chair. The gentle Christian presence she emitted was quite profound, but something I had never experienced. Decades later, daddy passed away in 2013.

At the funeral in Birmingham, the Harshes walked up to me, apparently seeing the twelve-inch hermetic cross tattoo on my leg. I just had it done, believe it or not, without knowing Daddy was going to die.

Mrs. Harsh asked, "Are you a Christian?"

And I said, "Yeah." And they were just elated.

She surprised me by revealing, "We had always prayed for your family. This is an answer to our prayers!"

I didn't know what to say. But nobody else got it. Except mom, when she got Alzheimer's, she started crossing herself.

And the rabbi would say, "You can't do that."

She'd go, "Yeah, I can."

So, this is how the journeys find us. But when I tell those two stories, I feel like I'm an ant among giants. Because how that happened, I don't know. And to this day, I feel almost sick thinking if that hadn't happened, both those things, where would I be? Now that said, Christianity, Judaism, Islam, those are all valid religions.

But they're not mine. Mine was to be Christian. So, how do I judge for others? There is no greater man than my father, who lived and died a devout, reformed Jewish man—devout, wonderful, community leader who built much of the city of Birmingham. You see how these things find us? They are the miracles. They're natural occurrences happening in an unusual way.

And I've had other things along my life, other people that were in my life at that time that I didn't know were praying for me. I had no idea.

Chapter 15:
Embracing Your Free Will

God gives us experiences but does not tell us what to do with them. That, my friend, is our job. The great Masters of Wisdom will not get the train going for us, but they'll certainly give it gas once we're on our way. Free will graces us with opportunities to choose right from wrong, love from hate. That about covers all experience. Remember the Invictus poem by William Ernest Henley, which states:

"Out of the night that covers me,
Black as the pit from pole to pole,
I thank whatever gods may be
For my unconquerable soul."

It finishes with, "I am the master of my fate, I am the captain of my soul." That powerful poem addresses free will trials and the effort we must exert to exceed. Do you often feel overwhelmed by the sheer effort required to persevere, to try? I sure do. Occasionally, I need a big timeout, which most folks consider a vacation. This might be an appropriate time to tell you that I was a very serious kid. I'm still serious, but I get lost in thought more than I admit, requiring a reality check to bring me back to focus.

I prefer small gatherings on occasion, but do not party (that's the verb). I neither drink nor do I choose to do any drugs of any sort, and I practice a dietary and exercise regimen that scares even me sometimes. I am light-hearted until someone loses control from substances, which means two drinks or any drug. Bye! No one invites us anywhere because Thom and I don't drink. We still have a great life. This allows much time for work and meditation, which I do find more valuable in the long run.

My free will redo is at the monastery called the Sacred Heart Retreat Center in Colorado. It's a silent retreat. I go to morning mass, walk the grounds, check in with my soul, my lost pieces, create art, and write. My cell, which is a tiny plain room with the usual monastic sink, bed, crucifix, and dresser. That's it. It's absolute bliss to me. So simple. Meals are silent; the hallways are silent, and the quietude is heaven. I love to go to the monastery for five to seven days.

If you travel to another time zone, be aware that it will take you 72 hours to fully be immersed in it. You will bring to that time zone energies from the last one. Likewise, when you return home, you carry the signature of that other place for 72 hours.

What if I told you that everything is planned, that it's known from the beginning to the end, but also that your choices using your own free will can change the plan? Both are true. Would you change how you live? How would you choose? I think we are absolutely too dumb and unable to recognize that dichotomy is a truth. It actually blows me away. The dumb part is simply a missed step in the ladder of evolution. We cannot flip back and forth between the idea that all is planned but that we also have free will. We just don't get it, along with the other truths we don't get. Maybe, just not yet. Will we evolve into a population who intuitively feel the difference is truth? I think humanity is on that path.

I have hope. I'm trying. We cannot theorize or intellectualize that truth; trusting the process is the theosophical path. I'll try that for a while. Let me know what you think. What if I told you I experienced that trust as an activity of trusting that I will be led, that all that I need to do is step into it? I experience a soft dance to the music of spirit. It feels like spirit guides me in the moment, and I step into the space created. In Theosophy, we say that humans must do 51 percent before spirit helps us.

I found that to be true in my life. During the Hurricane Katrina catastrophe, I heard a dark joke focusing on the misunderstanding of action versus waiting and free will. A certain population believes in the dogma that we should just trust and don't do anything because God will take care of you. I just don't buy that. So, here's the story. You've probably heard it, but I'm going to repeat it because it really makes sense to me. A man sat on the roof of his flooded home, watching the neighbors being rescued by boat.

When the rescuers came to him and asked him if he was ready to leave, he responded, "No, God will save me." As all these jokes go, the man repeated this scenario three times. Come nightfall, he drowned and found himself at the pearly gates facing God.

"Lord, I've been such a devout believer all of my days, but you let me drown."

The Lord responded, "But I sent three boats."

In my young and dumb years, which endure even through my 30s, my ego let go of any help unfamiliar to my prideful way of living. A lot of the boats passed through my life without me even recognizing them. How do we recognize the boats? I think we have to have been so disappointed in our failures to reach a zero point.

Humility is flawed. It can be false or hidden, rarely apparent until the end. Perhaps humility comes with age. Trust in spirit and the divinity of that dichotomy may be our starting point. I believe I'll die in the body unrepentant and comically climbing onto that roof and left out unless I learn more about my soul.

True good and evil are not present in the physical plane. The energy behind the events predates the kindness and compassion shown to another, generated from the timeless bounty of love within the bosom of the universal mind. The hateful evils done to others produce only more hate. Hate has a beginning and an end, while love is eternal. How can that be? Can we choose? Of course. Hate only stops love, while love continues to reproduce itself. Hate becomes nothing, and evil depends upon love to oppose it. Our free will can choose between love and hate. You are love, and you are loved: You need it most when you feel it the least. You are nothing but love expressed in flavors, colors, emotions, and feelings.

Love who you are and be who you are. God's will is sacrosanct. Our job is to connect our free will to His. That happens from the soul. We have to act. The Masters say try. It appears that the effort of showing our free will, shoving our free will into time and form absolutely creates and changes the outcome. Fate, astrology and numerology charts all of these are on autopilot. If we do nothing, that's what happens. What is the purpose of life if we refuse to participate, refuse to enact our free will to try? How can we be sure that God's will is what we connect to and create? We cannot. We really know fully that we are working towards the most spiritually beneficial outcome.

So, what's the point? The point is the effort itself, the try. We are here to spiritualize matter, and matter is under the influence of the dark lords. If satanic energy rules the world, we slide beyond its reach when we try and connect through prayer. And seeing what we can feel is the best plan. Does it guarantee success? No, but we shine when we try. By now, you're wondering what I do for fun. My life is my joy, and my work is my joy. There is nothing else I prefer to do.

I breathe it and create it daily. Are you also wondering what this has to do with free will? I'll tell you. Free will is the freedom we have to choose. It's my scene. It may seem that we have no choice at times, but if we back it up to how we got there in the first place, the genesis of the seed is choice. There it is. Free will is sacrosanct. It breathes through us like the Holy Spirit. When the most precious gift He gave us to live life on Earth is exposed, it is free will.

zoliartexoticamontana.com/music
"May The Road Rise Up To Greet Ye"

Your Questions Answered: How do I know why I am here?

Figuring out who you are and what you're doing, even if it's just a millisecond a day, everything counts. And that's all the Masters want for us is to try. They won't be the car, but they'll be the gas once we get going. In your life, being a thinking person, you will find that if you do things a certain way, your life is more pleasant, and that allows us when the shitty times come to be a little more balanced, at least a little more.

My husband is 6'4", 280 pounds, and I call him a big bad guy; I mean, this is a big dude. Thom trains SWAT teams and is a retired Tier One Operator. We are different kinds of human beings. He and I are nothing alike in 90 percent of our life. We are so different. But what we have done is learn who we are. And then we found the common spaces with the love and allowing each other to be who they are. And that is really what life is. Every time we walk out of this house, we're encountering something that we don't know about. The more we are ourselves, the more that we're going to be able to manage that.

But we have to have good boundaries, too. There's this weird dichotomy between having really good boundaries and being compassionate with other people. And I'm still learning, but it works for me when I maintain my boundaries. I allow other people to have theirs, too. In other words, this is my line in the sand. You can do anything you want over there, but once you cross mine, we're going to have words. It's very hard for codependent people; I call myself a recovering helpaholic. The people who knew me twenty years ago wouldn't even recognize me as who I am now. I'm so different.

Chapter 16:
Robin Hood Was An A–hole

    Stealing from the rich to give to the poor activates the polar opposite of wealth and poverty. Robin Hood's character was rebellious, plutonic in nature. He rebelled against the Sheriff of Nottingham, desiring to hurt his forcefulness by forcing him to lose what he guarded, meaning the role of guarding those he deemed worthy of the sheriff's attention. Rebellion activates force, not power. The renegade is inherently powerful from within, reacting and responding to external circumstances from his own intuitive sense of ethics.

    But the rebel's only allotment is in the creation of opposition to the existing force he deems to be wrong. Stealing from the rich accomplishes nothing in the long run. What does it change? Robin Hood could have educated the rich using his wily intelligence to gain the humility and heart-focused behavior of sharing what they had in excess. Sharing is done by those who feel in whose natures are evolved enough to nurture the sharing from their heart to the hearts of others.

Sean Penn is an example of a modern renegade. I say that because during Katrina, in Ukraine, and in a couple of other world trauma situations, he just went there. He said, I'm not going to talk about this. I'm going to physically go and help. He showed up. And that's an ideal of the renegade: Physically showing up and not hiding from the law. Now, I'm not saying that Sean Penn is perfect, but the idea of becoming involved in something for service and you just stay engaged. Instead of saying, I'm just going to take from these other people to get back at them because the other people don't learn anything.

Look what Desmond Tutu did. Now, there is a renegade right there. When apartheid ended in South Africa, Desmond Tutu forgave the offenders, who had actually hurt people. He said, "We're not going to punish you because you don't learn anything from that. We're going to forgive you, and we're going to love you because you didn't know any better." That's the ideal.

> *The Reality Pirate is a renegade who is authentic and knows it's okay to be different.*

We definitely need more of that in the world, and we have to start with ourselves. It's that new age prayer; I seek to heal, not hurt. And that's what it's about. In order to heal, we have to be temperate, and we have to hear God's voice. We have to wait. I'm going through some lessons with that right now with some people. To just wait, let it be uncomfortable. Just hold attention and see what happens with it.

It is tough. But I really can't say I'm a minister; I have to act like one. I mean, I am a minister, but if I don't act like one, what's the purpose? A big fat fake.

That authenticity is part of being a renegade. We aspire to these abstract ideals. I don't think we ever really fully get it. I think a rebel to me is a stop sign. A renegade is just a yield sign who is going to wait with behavior. They're just going to be themselves, and they may be a little confused as to why you think they're being weird. I'm just myself. I have a friend who's a counselor and she said this woman and her daughter came, and the woman said, "Why is my daughter always trying to be so different."

My friend had to say to the mom, in front of the daughter, "She's not trying to be different; she just is." That's the renegade.

It's okay for you to be different. You're here to be that person; embrace it.

Well, if we really are ourselves, we're all going to be different. Everybody's going to be a little special snowflake. But we try to join in society because we like to be together. Sometimes, we do sell ourselves short. We enact that archetype of the prostitute. And we do that for many different reasons. It's not a means to an end. It's not that it's so awful and evil. Sometimes we have to do that. Sometimes in order to be safe in the world, you really can't speak your truth. You kind of need to hide that. But that says a lot about the world, doesn't it?

So, what's a renegade to do when they don't feel safe speaking that truth?

It depends on the person. I think it depends on what we learn in childhood to keep ourselves safe. I have the opinion that if Thom and I get into a marital spat, and we will because if you're married, you're going disagree 70 percent of the time. You just have to learn, do it lovingly. Right? That's what our therapist says, and it's true. If we're in a marital spat, there are two nine-year-olds sitting there arguing. We each want our way. We feel defensive. We become these children who didn't know how to protect ourselves. And it's not that the adults were trying to hurt us; it's just that we wanted what we wanted.

I'm not sure the renegade and the rebel would react any differently. It depends on the person. During Katrina, I went to Olympia, and I did some work with the Red Cross. And we had people coming in who were big fat liars, and they were claiming checks that weren't theirs. So, the Red Cross had to put out a new booklet about how to deal with the fraud. I thought the new book was full of crap. So, I took the old one, and I went home and I called those people. I just left. I took it upon myself to call them and tell them that I knew what they were doing and that they had to stop. And apparently, they did.

I tend to just take things into my own hands and go, damn the consequences, I'm going to do what I feel is right. This is renegade behavior. Was I rebelling against that? Maybe I was. So, I'm not sure the behavior is really different in that particular sense. I think rebels are constantly rebelling against authority. And we do need people like that in the world.

A lot of them work in the political field. God help them. You know, without the dark, we really don't know the light. We live in the dark, and we seek the light, coming to Earth as an incarnation. I used to have a friend who said she had a birth memory coming through the canal thinking, "Oh, here we go again." Well, she was a character. She was a very interesting person. But we need all kinds.

How can we learn to be compassionate unless we're faced with assholes? We can't learn the good things unless we're faced with the bad ones. Otherwise, we'll never we'll never test ourselves.

Your Questions Answered: How to stop being an a-hole?

When you're young, you learn from others. And as you grow, you become more in tune with your own ability to see for yourself. That's generally how life works. The problem is, do we become so sure of ourselves that we're unable to learn from others? That's not good. That's the level of balancing confidence with humility, and it is a constant balancing act.

For example, if I know XYZ to be true and someone tells me their truth, am I willing to be empathetic to sit back and learn from their experience but still stay in my lane? There's no other way to gather information except to learn it or experience it, especially as younger people. I know my brother as a full professor and as a teacher; he is just a master at presenting information. And then the kids have to learn it and shoot it back at him. Then, at some point they have to give their own interpretation of that. But how can we give an interpretation of anything, a theory and understanding of spiritual truth, until we have gotten some boundaries with it, some parameters?

It really never ends. My insecurities as a person make me want to push my values if I'm unsure rather than listening or allowing others to help me with that. So, it's a balancing act. It's just human nature.

A really good observation about how insecurities reveal even more truths is our personality. In the ray structures of the body, we have a personality ray, which is what we come here for. It changes every lifetime. We come in to experience that. It's the emotional mess that we have to live in life. It's just miserable because we never really get it. We just don't ever really figure it out.

It's that backpack of seven deadly sins. It lives in the personality and the emotions because it's certainly not attached to the soul. The intellect can pretty much figure it out and detach from it. The physical body, whatever ray structure you have in the physical, that's what your brain will be. Most people are 3, 7, or 1. A 2 Ray body is like Charlie Chaplin, very fragile.

A 3rd Ray brain will be practical. A 5 Ray body will be scientifically oriented. We could go on and on about that. That's a whole other book.

In *Maitreya's Mission*, Benjamin Creme and his Master addressed that. That's a great read. It's three volumes of that kind of stuff. But see, there's an example right there. I spent twenty years reading and rereading those books dozens of times, and every time I open it up, I learn something different because I'm different than I was when I started reading. So, we do learn, and we do grow, but we have to do it on our own terms, and we're all just horribly impatient with everybody else's pace.

Welcome to Earth. There is no way to get past it until you evolve to where the soul is feeding you more than the personality. It takes thousands and thousands of lifetimes to get to that initiation. It takes thousands of lifetimes. That's why, I think, the world is in the state it's in. Most people have not taken the first-degree initiation. I don't want to get into all that. But the only the only help is prayer, meditation, and service because that activates the soul.

We basically have to be more gentle with each other, too. That would be nice. I think we have to start with ourselves on that because I noticed with myself, I tend to treat others how I treat myself. Over the years, I've calmed my mind and my impulsiveness down quite a bit. I tended to treat myself better. I think it's aging. I can't do what I did before. I can do what I do now, but I have to be more patient about that, and I move more slowly. So, I notice more.

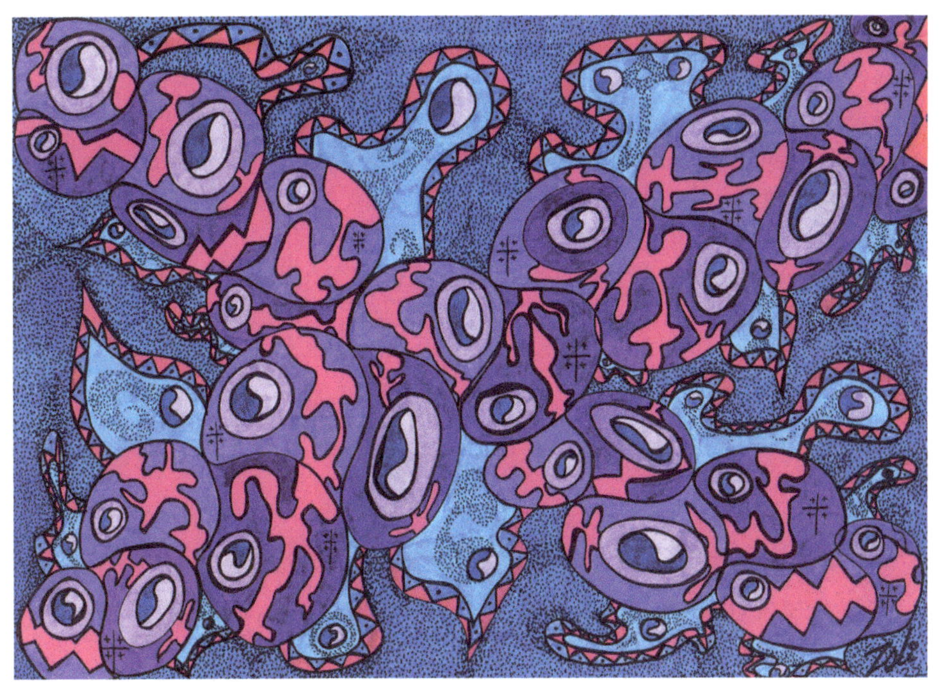

Chapter 17:
To Live by The Tides

Our grandson's other grandpa is Papa Nick. He's a Greek fisherman. He comes from a long line of Greek fishermen. They live in Olympia, Washington. He says he lives by the tides. That gracious, gentle sway of natural rhythm enthralls me. On Puget Sound in Olympia, breathing in the salt air and loving the same multi-generational lifestyle brought to this country. Who are we, my friend, and how do we press forward the gifts of our forefathers?

This great country is the New Jerusalem. See USA cradled in the middle of that name. We take in those beholden to their past culture with the freshness of American potential. The gnarled hands, furrowed brows, and bent backs of those who for so long pained to be stronger and more brilliant than their past. These are the new Americans. In future times, perhaps, not so distant, you'll be able to recognize the visage and coloring of an American as we do now recognize say, a Frenchman, or a Korean, or a person of color.

I imagine we will be rather tan, with different colored eyes and perhaps darker hair. Standing next to a Swede, we will say, "Oh, that's an American." The experiment set by hierarchy, the plan of light, and love is that the USA is indeed the melting pot. We become what we were and who has come here. England, on the other hand, is a different kind of experiment. The tides they live by is another story. In England, folks of different races and countries of origin habitat rather peacefully in their own respected lifestyles and customs.

> *My own prayers for peacefulness and love allow the God-given natural tides to calm our seas and invite in the other ways, strengthening its own diversity and love.*

The Asian community, the East Indian community, the Caucasians, and Celtics rarely intermingle in marriage, but they are congenial in commerce and greeting. Of course, there are exceptions, as nature tenderly presses into form the exception to the norm, just to keep things interesting. Here in the USA, what are the tides we live by? My own prayers for peacefulness and love allow the God-given natural tides to calm our seas and invite in the other ways, strengthening its own diversity and love.

zoliartexoticamontana.com/music
"Going Aloat"

Your Questions Answered: Should we follow certain tides more than others, or do we even have a choice?

Well, that's a sticky question because I think it's a dichotomy. I think God plans everything from the beginning. I'm not a scholar, but I think the Christian bible says that the end is known from the beginning. I think there's a certain day and time that we are destined to die and to be born. All of this is written in the stars, but also, we have free will. Those things, they seem totally opposite, but I don't think they are.

The key is to follow the tide. The tide was made by God and it's a rhythm that allows order. And that's Capricorn, that's Saturn, it allows order. And we can fit into that rhythm. If we ask God, higher power, what is His will for us in this life, and when we stay in our lane, if we can be patient, reticent, sharpen our mind, not be drugged out; all that stuff adds up. Once we have His will as our will, that's how we follow that tide.

We say we want God's will, and if God isn't fast enough, we turn to the other side. We go right into the deadly sins. Oh, well, he's not quick enough, and I want it now. That's not following the natural rhythm or living by the tides.

God makes the tides, and I think we're supposed to try. We see so many things as us messing up, but they're really just us trying. I'm very hard on myself. It's just awful. I really am, but I have that cancer moon, the cancer south node. I'm very sensitive. And I'm emotional. So, my challenge is to try to waylay some of those emotions. And what I've been saying to myself lately is, "Zoli, nothing you see happening out there or nothing that is said to you—none of this stuff has any emotion attached to it. Except what you put in it."

I'm chewing on that, and I have to remind myself about that. So that's where I am. And I think that goes with the tide coming in or out. We have to be aware of whether the tide is in or the tide is out. Astrology addresses that, numerology addresses that, these different psychic sciences stress that sometimes things are out, and sometimes they're in.

It's just part of human nature. My father used to talk about that. I would go from zero to sixty in just a second. He said, "As you grow up and as you age, you will find you don't go all the way to that side. You'll go a little more towards the middle. Then sooner or later, you will be able to stay in the middle."

That took me sixty years to learn. And it depends on what kind of person you are and what kind of tide you have. If the tide comes in and takes away everything that you value, you have to reassess it. Some people's tides come in and out with ease, like my husband, who is a very lucky person. It's in his astrology; his numerology; he's just lucky. And he has the most bizarre stuff happen. I think, how does that happen? Well, that's how God has set his life because he has earned that in the past. But his tides come in a little more gently than mine that come in like tsunamis. When people look at my astrology chart, most of them say, what were you thinking? What the hell?

We are honored to be on the planet in this lifetime because this is the lifetime that I believe the world teacher, Maitreya, is going to come out into the open. We will see the beginnings of world peace. We will see the correction of our environment. This is it. This lifetime is huge.

Twenty-six years ago, when I went through my Hunka adoption on the Rosebud Res, we became family. During the Sundance festival they have annually, the heyoka comes out. This is a person who is dressed like a weird clown. The heyoka will say everything backwards. Like, I hope you have a horrible life, and I hope nothing works for you. This is because they believe it will tease the spirits into thinking to do the opposite. Life is like that. And I think we can accept that heyoka energy.

It's connected to the *Wakinyan*, which are thunder beings, and they bring change. It's fire. If you are destined to do your work, why do you expect not to burn up occasionally or have to start over? We just forget. And that's the value of the astrology chart, numerology chart, and Theosophy. All these paths remind us to look at the heyoka and say that we will have hard lives, which will be unbearable sometimes. Why do you expect it to be easy? You see? That's one of my main messages, and I'm telling you, it's not popular with me or anybody else.

Chapter 18:
Ritualized Crone

I am a ritualized crone. Aging is an evolving mystery to me as I reinvent myself with helpful adaptations to an aging physical body. I no longer ride quads like a banshee on holiday, nor do I exercise to a maximum level. My mother would applaud that I have finally embraced some moderation and conscious balance.

The three stages of female embodiment are the maiden, the mother, and the crone. It's that third one that stumps us Westerners. Let me clear some of this up for you because I know you are as confused as I was when my crone years began.

The crone is the wise woman archetype. It presents as the older women complete with mid-age hope that we'll find a way to prolong youthfulness. Even a great plastic surgeon and hormone therapy cannot return that image to us. So, what is a girl to do? I was blessed with a kick-ass mother who marched me to an esthetician when puberty emerged on my face at age 14. Mrs. Snow educated me in skin care and nutrition, the sage advice I totally ignored by baking in the Florida sun and acting the fool.

I found my healthful balance only gradually as I immersed myself in herbology, homeopathy, and exercise. But the reality of cronehood smirks at effort unless that effort is grounded in the maiden or mother years of healthy habits. When does crone hood begin? The image is an old gnarled woman stirring the pot with other Macbethian witches. Wisdom does not demand decay but commands a wise acceptance of the aging process. I'm still challenged in that. Cronehood begins sometime after the initiation of menopause.

> *Something magical happens when the woman breathes that last breath of midlife youth and begins to accept and explore her final journey towards counsel and sharing her skills with younger women.*

I did not feel like a crone until I hit 63. Something magical happens when the woman breathes that last breath of midlife youth and begins to accept and explore her final journey towards counsel and sharing her skills with younger women. That acceptance melts all hope and illusion of returning to a phase when she could use her youthfulness to get her needs and wants met. We use what we have, don't we? It is indeed a man's world when women focus only on prolonging appearance instead of increasing wisdom and joy within.

How long can the second Saturn return affect a croning? For quite a while actually. The wisdom has a sort of time release capsule attached. The second return falls somewhere in between the age of 56 and 60. For men, it's also a marker of that final era where peace of mind comes from learning to give back, to become more of a soul than a personality. But we'll delve into the astrology thingy later on. You're going to like this!

Any ego-generated thoughts confuse God's heart-centered quietude and subtle offerings to my free will of choice. I am His, and He is mine. Many gal friends balk at my identifying as a Montana housewife, even though this profession is my bliss in cronehood. If one were to follow me down around daily, one would observe an old southern-bred woman caring lovingly for her home, her husband, her animals, her health in a Cancerian occupation of home and hEarth.

My Zoliart work, the triplets of music, art, and writing, is a joy and a gift to me from God. When I follow my intuition, I find myself turning left when my logic demands that I turn right.

Plans lay fallow as intrigue often guides my decisions, seemingly haphazardly and unprepared. Unbeknownst to my logical self, unsure of the next step, I forage through the material world as if bent on insanely following what I do not know is there. Common sense, logic, left brain planning are replaced with a sense of not knowing what is coming and being okay with that. That's intuition to me. The intuitive mind differs from the logical mind in those ways.

I often find myself questioning why I am in a certain place or why I'm drawn to say something in a particular way. The unexpected becomes the ordinary. It's all in my state of mind, a synthesis of heart and mind. It's attunement to a specific frequency in an ocean of waveforms and seemingly endless possibilities. If I remain within the aura of the attunement, synchronicities occur moment by moment. If I remain aware of my very awareness, I am able to ride the wave into the next experience.

There is no time there. Time expands laterally rather than forward and back. In 1978, I developed some theories while working with my NASA physicist buddy, Dr. Adrian B. Clark, in Huntsville. We had an uproariously fun ten years of banging heads against presumed truths and unprovable theories. One of them was my "lateral reality manipulation theory." It addresses the present point of expansion, ballooning out from a center point that negates temporality when we are in the moment.

Everything simply is. Time expands to the left and right rather than to the future or, memorably, in the presumed past. When we are present in the moment, experience becomes fat and full. Those intuitive synchronous moments when time stops are a real truth. I have to stay out of my head. I don't think about what my intuition is doing. We create from the three centers; head, gut, and heart. Intuition breathes through the heart; it is not a neural or a thought process. It is the color, not the form. The flavor, not the cake itself.

zoliartexoticamontana.com/music
"All The Girls I Know Are Fat"

Your Questions Answered: Why do some women avoid the ritualized crone?

It seems to be repressed a lot, and people are always trapped by aging. I don't know if that's a loss of wisdom or just not recognizing it. I think it's always there. Sophia is the wisdom in the archaic Jewish way of looking at things, the Old Testament's way, Theosophy. It's always there; we just have to access it. So, the crone in American society is just not done because we associate it with the witches of Macbeth or women looking awful. In Western society, women aren't allowed to look awful and still be valid.

That is changing a lot, and I'm thrilled to see it. I think this new Barbie movie has come out. I don't plan on seeing it. But she's pretty much kick ass, and she pretty much owns it. So, I think croning will be more accepted. There are more TV shows of women not loaded with makeup, with all the hair, the whatever, and we all look like that at times. So, I think it's more realistic. The crone is something that the women don't want to be and the men don't want to see.

I think in other societies, in the ancient societies, cronism and older people are so much more revered. And as a country, we're just young and dumb. That's all there is to it. We'll figure it out sooner or later, but nobody moves faster than this country itself in the United States. Canada is very close behind it. We came here to this country to bring change. It is the New Jerusalem. And a lot of it's just done wrong. It is going to take time for women to find more of who we are for the wisdom of the crone to rise up.

Chapter 19:
The Warrior and The Priest

Thom and I sat with our grandson, Liam, watching *The Lion King*. Neither Thom nor I had seen the new version but smiled when the same songs filled the room with memories of years past. My psychic intuitive process is usually triggered by a visual or auditory stimulus. It feels like downloads deposit fully formed, and all I have to do is write them down. Sometimes, my writing is so fast that I can barely read it myself. When I review transmissions without the auditory signal, the visuals are always there.

I see words and brightly colored images accompanied by full-bodied feeling. When I'm driving in a car, I can't exactly pull it over to the shoulder to write, so I try to make note of a few keywords to recall the download. In the 1970s and 1980s, when I was working with the Zeta Reticuli on what they called interdimensional physics, these downloads came fast and furious. I could not go one hour without scribbling down the formulas, equations, and theories they projected into my mind.

I have a huge trunk load packed with this work. They told me just to keep it in a safe place. Several years ago, I connected with my dear friend and colleague, Ray Hernandez, who compiled research and experiences in his book *Contact Modalities*. We discussed how the group of us, scientists and experiencers, all received that peculiar signature of interdimensional physics language. It's just crazy we didn't even know each other. Oh boy, am I off-topic.

Let's return to *The Lion King*. When Simba displayed his lack of confidence over not wanting to fight Scar for the kingship, I felt a flash of inspiration enter my heart. I saw the words, the warrior and the priest. As I snuggled up to my hubby, watching our young grandson enthralled with the wonder of digital cartooning, I jumped up to grab a pad and pen to write what I had come through. I bet you're wondering where I think all this came from. I theorized that my musical composition, my transmissions, my art, all of that stuff, they're all out there somewhere, and all I need to do is match a frequency to receive it.

Have you ever wondered why and how several people all over the world may get identical ideas, formulas, or inventions at the same time? Why do scientists who are far across the globe from each other sometimes invent the same things? In my understanding, everything kind of floats down into the Earth's atmosphere for us to pick it up. Maybe it's true that there's nothing new under the sun. But the new comes from beyond the sun.

Well, I know you're getting impatient about the Lion King thingy. Sorry. Here's the story I promised. The story that I received, called the warrior and the priest, reminds me of the story of Krishna and Arjuna on the battlefield. Arjuna, a member of a royal family, had to fight his family on the battlefield and didn't want to. Krishna reminded him that this was his karma, this was his duty to be who he came to be.

"You don't need to change who you are," began the priest to the warrior. "You simply have to just be who you are."

"What is that supposed to mean?" Asked the warrior.

The priest said. "It means that you are both a warrior and a priest."

You express one side of yourself, then the other. The yang and the yin, the outside and the inside; the enemy is the self, inside of the soul self. The warrior fights the enemy within, mirroring the enemy without. Your heart is your eternal soul, not your body, but your passing emotions. Be the priest and be the warrior, both at the same time.

My husband Thom, a retired JSOC operator, relates how they were trained to be warrior athletes. The priests within guided their extreme successes and development of almost superhuman abilities as the elite fighters for our country.

zoliartexoticamontana.com/music
"When I Become A Man"

Your Questions Answered: How do you find the balance between the warrior and the priest?

By being miserable. The way we find a balance to anything is by going too far in one direction. And then something happens. That warrior priest archetype is very prevalent and important for men. And I think that is part of what could come back for them. As a woman, I don't like it when I see TV commercials where they're making the man look like he's just a wuss. You don't have to do that to be powerful. You just need to honor the masculine.

Just think of Jason Momoa, an alpha male heartthrob. He is a happy guy and a powerful male image. Well, you don't have to make that kind of man weak in order for you to be strong. You don't want that.

The warrior priest story addresses men. It says when you are younger, go off and make your mark; hunt things, write things, build things. Men have to see the efforts of their work. The physical world is how they are because men are more external, women are more internal. But men will reach that point where they can no longer be the warrior. They have to be more priestly, and that's the male crone.

These are powerful archetypes, and I would like to see some sort of healthy resurgence for men. I know there are groups that do that. And I think there have been male movements that have done that. But of course, they all devolve into sex and alcohol, and it's just ridiculous. This powerful male image has definitely been diminished over time, especially in media.

If you look at who's writing the media, Hollywood is very fashionable. It wants to belong. It's absolutely awful. I think that it'll change around, but it's almost like the abused becomes the abuser. That's an old statement we use in recovery. When the abused become the abuser, there is a mentality that if we can't be powerful women, we'll get together and we'll diss men.

We figure it out, but I think the main thing to say is that the abused becomes the abuser. And that's always violent. I grew up in the Old South, and some of my nannies, these goddesses that raised me, their parents were slaves as children. They were born in the eighteen hundreds. One of these women was Pernie Thomas, who worked with us when I was a child, and she couldn't read or write.

She was just amazing; she came out of the cotton fields. This is our era of the Old South. Now when they had Black Lives Matter, a good idea was taken and became violence and hating people. And the people that started Black Lives Matter are now multi-millionaires with big houses, still saying that they're victims. This happens sometimes when the abused still holds on to the victim mentality and then abuses other people.

That is an awful situation. Nobody wins. There is no power. I love what Barack Obama said, "If you built that car, you didn't do that by yourself. We do nothing by ourselves." It's a perfect statement to say. It is true. He is an example of the first black president to give hope to these young black kids so they can see possibilities for themselves.

So, we don't have any of it right in this country, but the Masters tell us not to worry; we will figure it out. Everything's in alignment. I think when we address the cause, when we keep backing stuff up, we discover how this happened. We'll back it up and back it up, then we can see it.

And that's wisdom. That's the priest, and that's the crone. And the image of the priest or the crone is somebody who is reticent, who's not going to jump and have an emotional hissy fit because they didn't get their way.

Chapter 20:
What Comes Next?

Back in the early 1990s, at my farm, I had a plethora of blueberries and fruits. I invited the gleaners out to pick the fruits and to take them to nursing homes and people in need. The cleaners were a delightful group of women and men, probably my age now or older, that'd be seventy years old. A gentleman came out one day, a gnarled, delightful character, smoking a cigarette, holding a can of Coke.

He said to me. "Hi, I'm Bob from George."

I said, "From George? You mean the gorge? Or is there a George Washington?"

He said, "No, I'm from the planet George."

Bob looked to be maybe ninety years old, and I had never met anyone who claimed to be from another planet who was not perhaps ten years old. I said, "Okay, tell me about that."

Bob went on to say that there were many planets that were habited. I had never heard that or didn't really believe it yet. He said, "I'm from a planet called George." So, to honor Bob, I asked him, to write me some articles for the Reality Pirate newsletter. I'm including one here, well, just to tell you a bit about him and to honor him.

Bob and Kathy are both gone now to other worlds and other realities in this year of 2023, but I love my friend, and I honor him. So, here's what he wrote.

What Comes Next by Bob from George

One of the attractions of science is that numbers and facts can be manipulated into patterns and become increasingly simple until one reaches a bottom level of simplicity that explains all the diverse data from which the simple formula has been distilled.

Our entire technology rests upon about a dozen simple formulas. Unfortunately, we haven't even begun to devise any parallel formulas for the confusing mass of seemingly uncoupled events that appear on television and in our daily newspapers. Even worse, no one seems to realize that such a distillation is possible or even worth thinking about. We take the view that human actions are randomized and, therefore, unpredictable events. To that, I say, a phooey.

In my own view, it is that every event, be it a brownie in motion of a subatomic particle of speech of a president, was inevitable from the moment time began. It was not predestined, which is what the Puritans would have you believing back around 1689, but inevitable because every action is also a reaction. But even if I'm correct, my theory doesn't help us predict the future nor understand the chaotic events of the universe. In analogy, we're sitting in the theater, watching the play of light and dark, thinking of ourselves in connection with all that's on the screen. We are so immersed in the action that our role as an audience becomes indistinguishable from that of a participant.

What bugs me is that I want a method of predicting what comes next, and I just don't have one. Not that there aren't several around. Emile Coué came up with the mantra which says, "Every day, in every way, things are getting better and better." Karl Marx came up with his historical imperative coupled with dialectical materialism. Nietzsche came up with his Superman. I dare say there are others. The problem is that they contradict each other. I can't put too much faith in any one of them. So, how do you cope with this problem? You, too, are a child of the Age of Reason that held all things to be amenable to logic.

You, too, are the product of a technological age. I won't accept a reply that you've never given the problem much thought. You may have not been put into quite the same context, but I know the problem disturbs you. If it didn't, you'd be as serene as the Buddha, which I expect you aren't. In spite of my inability, however, I have begun to act on my assumption of inevitability.

There's no way to raise the crops without plowing the ground.

During the last week or so, the rains have been falling here about and the public has been grousing about the so-called lousy weather in western Washington. Nonetheless, I've been amused by raising my hand

and intoning my most in my most sepulchral voice, "The good lord sent the rain to make the flowers grow." Faces showed a momentary surprise followed by an embarrassed guilt. They nodded or said yep or some such, at which I smiled and said in my sweetest voice, "There's no way to raise the crops without plowing the ground." What relevance this has to the fact that the rain is still falling, I don't know, but the statement is always received as if it had come from the lips of a prophet.

I'm trying to come up with a parallel statement to rationalize the 114-degree heat that we get during the summer here. Maybe it's to make the cactus grow. I confess my formula does not get down to human events. Earthquakes, floods, tornadoes, and plagues of locusts I can rationalize, but what humans do is beyond my understanding. Since no other discipline has shed much light on my dilemma, I've turned to sociology. The textbooks are full of things we all know, which doesn't get us very far ahead of what we already are, where we already are.

The closest I've come thus far is to develop a sort of algebra of intersections, which is a matrix in which decisions are made on dichotomous situations. It's a nice way of tracing back to see how the plot developed before I came into the theater, but it doesn't enliven the future. Well, maybe I'm wrong, but I still think that there's an underlying explanation of such universal phenomena as a drop in the stock market, the serving of beer only at state functions in Tanganyika, the invasion of Laos, and the demand of East Pakistan for independence from West Pakistan.

The problem is to find it. So, I have to tell you that Bob from George, his name was Bob Lunch, and his delightful wife Kathy were dear souls. Bob was around my life during the same era that I was receiving interdimensional physics from the Zeta Reticuli. We'll talk about that a little bit later, but here I had a guy standing in front of me who said he was from out there. It was too irresistible not to become a dear friend with Bob from George.

Your Questions Answered: What brings you hope?

The stars. I know what is coming. If I feel hopeless, or if I feel down and dejected, all I have to do is remember that we're eternal; we never die. All that dies is physical, and we are eternal. We were created to live forever in these states of consciousness. And that's what does it for me. There's no other way to address it. We have to accept that everything of this physical world has a beginning, a middle, and an end.

That's a hard thing to deal with. Because the body itself, the physical body doesn't want to die. It'll hold on. It just has fear attached to it. But my hope is in the stars. It's to know that we came from there and to there we will return. And that there is nothing on this Earth that lasts except love.

How do we become more loving? What if I say to you, "I love you."

I do. I love you. You don't owe me. I don't owe you. I really do love people. I feel an intense love for humanity. I don't have to like their behavior, and there are plenty of people I don't want to be around, but I can love them. Because it's something different. It's a state of being more than a state of mind. It never goes away.

Every single person out there is a spark of God. Every single person, no matter how brilliant, how foul, how loving, how hateful, it's all God.

But it's true. So, love is the answer to every damn thing we ask about. How can I do this to be more loving? If Thom, my husband, and I have a marital spat, how can we be more loving and forgiving to the other person? How can we say, you know what, I hope that when I mess up next time, you will love me enough and be able to help me? And I got a great guy. I mean, Thom's wonderful, what he has to put up with. How would you like to have to live with me? It would drive you crazy. I'm not always fun. I'm intense.

He's so laid back and so cool. He is this big bear of a guy, and I am like this little Jack Russell terrier. But love is the answer, and our misinterpretation of love is what the problem is. If you walk up to somebody and say, "How are you today? I love you." They'll look at you like you had a dick growing out of your forehead.

People are afraid of love, and they do misinterpret what it means. We all crave it so much that if somebody says, "I love you," the natural response is "Oh, good. You're going to give me what I want in life." No. They're not.

My quest is to help people see that human nature is a vast and continuous experience of messing up. It's just what we do, and I demonstrate that in my work, in my art, my music, whatever, that really, we're just people. We can't help it. We're just dumb.

It really does come back to learning how to love better. I don't know if I'll ever figure it out, but I'll keep trying. I really do want people to feel they're okay with a lot of this. I can't fix the world, but maybe it can make a difference somewhere.

Conclusion

All things of this world have a beginning, a middle, and an end. Our lives circle around each other, and we come to terms, eventually, with our own roles in all three aspects. The cause creates the effect. The beginning begets the end. My prayer for you is that your heart be strengthened with the courage called upon to fight the good fight, to love the dearest of your karmic relations and that you fall into a deep dark hole which eventually leads you to the strength and illumination to dig out of the mysteries hidden within.

Is it peculiar to wish that others devolve into the depths? Only if I were to assure you that you would remain stuck in them, but I don't. I believe in you. When I fell into such a space and shamanically journeyed to see Chiron ferrying souls across the river Styx, steering me in his skiff only revealed to me that he demands a real actual coin for passage across the abyss separating life from life. Chiron showed me that Caesar's world is our school while we are alive in a body, to render to Caesar what is his and to God what is God's.

That real coin was the last material demanded, a transfer of consciousness to the next plane. I collect memento mori skulls. I've got a lot of them. They remind me of the experience of all the physical life. In the monasteries of old, the little empty room one entered upon as one arrived into the monastery displayed only a lone skull on a table. Enter here all you who dare to leave illusion behind. I end this humble book with a prayer that your journey be difficult and fraught with the dangers presented to increase your love, your light, and your power. May your Guardian at the gate terrify you with the impossible demand that you give up your personality to your soul. I know you can do this. I believe in you, and I love you.

From the point of light within the mind of God, let light stream forth into the minds of men. Let light descend on Earth. From the point of love within the heart of God, let love stream forth into the hearts of men. May Christ return to Earth. From the center where the will of God is known, let purpose guide the little wills of men, the purpose that the Masters know and serve. From the center that we call the race of men, let the plan of love and light workout, and may it seal the door where evil dwells.

Let light, and love, and power restore the plan on Earth.

As above, so below. As it is written, so shall it go. As it is spoken, so will it be. Love is the law through eternity. So, mote it be.

Run with scissors. Zoli Althea

zoliartexoticamontana.com/music
"The Lord's Prayer Aramaic"

Salmon and Raven

zoliartextocamontana.com/music
"Salmon and Raven"

Acknowledgements

Thank you to the collaborators who helped in the creation of this book.

Photographic Art:

Peaceful Simplicity is all about encouragement and enjoying the simplicity that peace brings. I live on the east coast of Canada and I love to photograph God's creation. I use the beauty of nature as the backdrop to bring words of encouragement to a world of turmoil, fear and confusion. It is my hope that in some small way it can make a difference. Please visit www.peacefulsimplicity101.com for more.

The Olympia Project CD cover image was taken by Stephanie Austin at ecoastrology.com

Graphic Design:

Tristin is an aspiring artist who enjoyed drawing the Reality Pirate. He was inspired by the artwork he saw in indie games like Hollow Knight and later became interested in character design after playing Banjo-Kazooie. He can be reached at tristindesigns64@gmail.com

Editing:

Linda Beaulieu is an editor and project manager who lives in the forest with her family in Canada. She loves collaborating and helping people share there stories. Contact her at: lindasusanbeaulieu@gmail.com

Formatting:

Trisha Fuentes is a Top-Rated Freelancer on Upwork who offers book formatting and custom book cover design. Contact her at: ardentartistbooks@gmail.com

Request other books in the Reality Pirate Series from your favorite eBook retailer:

The Reality Pirate's Journal: A Thesis on the Nature of Things

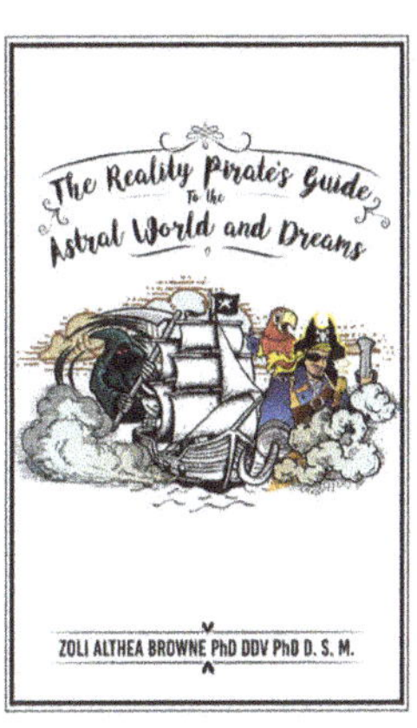

The Reality Pirate's Guide to Dreams and Astral Travel

Visit ZoliArt for more music, art, and writing:
zoliartexoticamontana.com

Disclaimer

These writings and the content of this book are the property of ZoliArt Companies, LLC, its affiliated organizations and governing bodies, their members, managers, employees, agents or representatives (collectively, the "Owner") and represent the Owner's personal experiences and opinions. These writings and the content of this book are subject to copyright and may not be sold, transferred, copied, used, or reproduced in whole or in part without the prior written consent of the Owner.

These writings and the content of this book are neither legal, religious, medical, psychiatric, or psychological advice in any way, nor should they be interpreted as such if the reader chooses to adopt and employ any methods presented in this book. The information provided herein is general and not intended to address any specific issue or topic. The accuracy and completeness of information provided herein are not guaranteed or offered to produce any results, and the advice and strategies contained herein may not be appropriate for any one particular person or situation. The Owner shall not be liable for any loss incurred as a consequence of the application or use, directly or indirectly, of any information presented in these writings. The Owner is not responsible for the actions or failures of any third parties, nor is the Owner responsible for any advertisements or for any content linked to this book. The Owner makes no representation regarding the reliability of this book. Readers accept all risks. Any claim for damages shall be limited to the amount paid by the claimant to the Owner for services.

These works are presented to provide information only. It is the reader's responsibility to seek appropriate advice, including but not limited to advice from medical and legal professionals, before making any change in lifestyle or putting any information obtained from this site into practice. The Owner neither diagnoses illnesses, nor prescribes treatment. The information provided herein is not a substitute for medical care. The writings and content of this book may change at any time, with or without notice.

The Reality Pirate's Guide to Your Paranormal Normal
Copyright © 2024